Madmen Must

A  BOOK

Madmen Must

WILLIAM JOVANOVICH

1817

HARPER & ROW, PUBLISHERS

NEW YORK, HAGERSTOWN

SAN FRANCISCO

LONDON

The author acknowledges with gratitude the information he obtained on the early church fathers of the East from Robert Payne's *The Holy Fire* (Harper & Brothers, New York, 1957).

FIRST EDITION

Designed by Sidney Feinberg

Library of Congress Cataloging in Publication Data

Jovanovich, William.
Madmen must.
   I. Title.
PZ4.J86Las [PS3560.084] 813'.5'4   77–11543
ISBN 0–06–012247–1

78 79 80 81 82 10 9 8 7 6 5 4 3 2 1

To
Stefan Jovanovich
who helped me

"It is the end, going west. California is the end of the line," I said carefully.

"Then it can be no less than Utopia. One does not dream beyond the limit."

"Madmen must."

"They are here, too. It is the last place. It is also the last time."

Madmen Must

Chapter

1

Afterward, I remembered that Thomas Wolfe said nothing important happens at one o'clock in the afternoon. But only afterward. Then, in my usual fashion, I dressed my memory with a borrowing from books. The undertaker was not in the least unctuous. He was brisk but unhurried, a bald, sandy-colored man who wore rimless glasses and spoke in whole sentences. "We've taken care of many of your father's people," he said. "I've dealt with your dad for years. He must be proud to have a son who finished college."

Was it condescension? Without being sure, I was resentful and must have shown it, for he went on to speak of his trade as between professionals. He leaned away from his desk, holding his feet to the carpet, and braced his fingers. What he said made it probable he assumed I had majored in business. "Small things can make or break policy." He smiled. "When I first joined Linklater's here they thought it peculiar that I insisted our hearses always take a different route back from the cemeteries, different, don't you see, from the way they go. I figure twice as many people see the company name and size up our equipage." He waited, and when I didn't say anything, he went on. "It's like the time I was with the Jaynes Company. I convinced them to spend extra to bind packages with double strands of string. A woman leaves the store, the string breaks, then she feels unsatisfied with shopping, which ought to be a pleasure. Small things like that work against you." The truth is that I was interested in what he said. I am always impressed by accounts of procedure, of how the world ordinarily gets through the day. I am a learner of facts and become restive on realizing that someone else knows things I do not.

When we finished the business of arranging the funeral, I went outside and stood on the corner to wait for a street-car. It was Thursday, one o'clock in the afternoon. The clear air was hot and literal. No one was on the street, no car passed by, and I didn't see a dog or a child. It was open and steady and still in the particular way of western cities, Salt Lake and Denver and Omaha. As I stood on the white cement sidewalk, I somehow became conscious of the plainness of time. There is no use to make yourself think, even on the occasion of a funeral, that things are inevitable when what they are, mainly, is typical. Standing in the white light of the afternoon, I realized that fatefulness has no quality. Inside those brick bungalows across the wide street, there could be lean old men in high-top shoes and their wives just sitting and waiting, not expectant, not wary.

My father buried Savo Lubradovich two days later in the low-lying ground of the old cemetery, not far from the meat-packing houses. The cemetery was not actually old, for in our city few places were built earlier than the remembrance of living people; rather, it had simply lost out to larger and better-kept cemeteries on the north side.

2

Because it was a working day, there were not more than thirty people standing before the open grave. Most of us looked, in the manner of our people, tall and drawn and fierce. The men wore black suits, some with white shirts buttoned to the collar but without neckties. When we shifted our feet it was with a respectful caution. Now and again one of us would look away from the priest to the dry bed of the river below and to the cottonwood trees on the other side. Once the priest had drawn the Orthodox crucifix in the air over the grave, one vertical line and two crossing, my father spoke in Serbian. He said that Savo's father had fought the Turks in the war of 1876, that Savo came to America in 1905 to work in the copper mines in Butte; he had gone back to fight in the First Balkan War, returned and worked some more and died, a long-time member of The Serbian People's Lodge. My father paused, looked at me standing at the foot of the grave, lowered his great head, his eyes showing nothing. I had never known him to pray: he was not preparing to do so now. When he resumed, I was sure he would conclude by scolding the survivors. As president of the lodge, my father conducted the burials of those members who were bachelors, as many Serb coal miners in America are. He ended the eulogy by noting that each year the lodge lost members.

"You're talking to the wrong people," I told him as we walked back to his car, our heels canting pebbles from the walkway onto the yellow-green grass. "These people already belong."

"I know, I know," he said. "Who else have I got to talk to?"

We stood at the car, side by side, leaning against the doors with a foot hitched on the edge of the running board, watching the other mourners walk away. Several stopped to shake my hand, especially those who had seen me infrequently since I went off to the university. The older women were confident in greeting me: our people like to celebrate young men. Soon they were all gone. At the grave two workmen moved squares of sod, but we could not hear them. The warm air deepened, intervened, so that before us everything looked distant. The cottonwoods across the creek were indistinct, their leaves flat like shadows against the branch lines.

"You remember Savo when you were a boy?" my father asked me in Serbian.

"Yes, of course I do. He seemed to me ten feet tall. I remember on Sundays when he came to visit he wore a gold chain across his vest with three or four rings hanging from it. His hands were as big as yours."

"He killed a man once in Hibbing, Minnesota. Nobody insulted Savo. He wouldn't permit it."

"What will you do with his money and things?" I asked, although I did not expect the answer to vary from the many previous instances.

"I'll send them to his sister in Niš. She'll get the bank draft and a bundle of his belongings all the way from America and after a while she'll get someone to write me to ask if there hadn't been more money." He said it without irony.

A slight stirring in the air reached us from across the creek. My father turned, put on his heavy pearl-gray hat, and opened the car door.

"I'd like to talk with you when we get back," I said to him.

"I know."

Ten days after Savo was buried I took the ferryboat that

crossed from San Diego to the island. The boat headed straight into a slip and the cars came off onto a wide boulevard that ran west toward the ocean for about two miles and then made a sweep to the south, turning back on itself to make a circle at the entrance to the hotel. The boulevard had two roadways separated by streetcar tracks on a mall, and it bisected the island so neatly that a stranger could comprehend the town at once. It was a fine arrangement for a summer place. Attached to the boulevard like fish ribs were side streets that curved away and tapered to the water's edge, which on the south, facing San Diego Bay, was lined with oil storage piers and warehouses. On the north there stood houses of white and blue and pink stucco with wide porches and long eaves, some of them so expensive it was improbable that they were occupied only seasonally. The houses were even larger near the oceanfront, at the far end from the ferry.

As the streetcar entered the big curve, I could see the massive white hexagon of the hotel, its brick-red dormers and corner turrets rising behind blue palms that here bordered the roadways. Everything typical of the town stopped at the hotel. Exiting from the circle in front of the hotel there was a narrow highway that ran down to the Mexican border. It crossed a causeway, then followed a spit of land between the ocean and South San Diego Bay. Scattered incidentally like beach grass off the highway were cheap houses made of weathered board set on brick stilts, shacks that sold fishing bait, small tourist cabins, and garages with flat fronts. Despite these mean buildings, the beaches on the spit were very good, in fact deeper and finer than those fronting the hotel.

I crossed the bay on a late afternoon when the ferryboat was almost empty. On the streetcar there were only a few passengers, including, to my surprise, two Filipinos. I got off a couple of blocks before the end of the line, at the start of the curve, and walked past expensive shops: I. Magnin, The May Company, others. On the right, just before the main entrance, was a sign that said: EMPLOYMENT OFFICE 10:00 A.M. TO 12:00 A.M. It was a single room at the bottom of the north façade of the hotel; above was green latticework that must close in, I assumed, the service entrances. A woman sat behind a narrow worktable on which there were card-file boxes and wire baskets. She was a small woman with darkened eyebrows, her hair pulled tight away from her forehead. I told her that a college friend said summer jobs were available for someone who had experience as a waiter.

"Have you got a union ticket?" she asked, and then answered her own question. "You would have to start in the dining room where the hotel staff eats." I had been forewarned at home to take this job without arguing for something better. The unions were strong in California, yet you could wait tables in the employees' dining room without a ticket because union waiters do not serve their own kind. "We can use a 'second waiter,' " she said. "You get only base pay because you get your meals here and can stay free at the hotel dormitory three blocks away." I told her I wanted the job after she said that it paid ninety dollars a month. "Of course," she said curtly but without malice, "there are no tips."

The work was simple. The employees' dining room was at the end of a long corridor leading from the kitchen, past the checker (who sat in a kiosk), past the double doors of the main dining room on the left and, on the right, farther down, the room-service waiters' call room. You took orders from the tables and walked the length of the corridor to the kitchen, which supplied the main dining room as well as the poolside terraces and room service. The only other place where food was prepared was in the cafeteria, directly below the main kitchen. After a day or two I could rank the employees from observing their eating drill. The important employees ate alone and were served by dining room waiters: the chef in a glass-walled room inside the main kitchen, the maître d' at a table set near a single door leading to the main dining room, the hotel manager in his main-floor office, and the housekeeper in her mezzanine room. Except for the room-service waiters—who frequently managed to steal the best entrées and eat on the run while still on duty—all the main hotel employees ate in the employees' dining room. The lowest grades, the second waiters and the janitors and the Filipino busboys, took their meals in the cafeteria below, where swordfish was usual.

Most of the help I waited on were not demanding. They talked very little, though they sat as peers, the receptionists together, the "social directors," the assistant headwaiters, the office clerks. The waiters alone were outspoken and pretended to a conspiracy of familiars, making up temporary nicknames for each other, and complaining repeatedly about the management. They speculated how much better the pay and tips were at the race tracks, Santa Anita and Del Mar, or at big Los Angeles hotels, the Huntington in Pasadena and the Beverly Hills. Though they were less obviously malcontent, the other employees at times acted averse, as if quarantined.

At first I didn't attempt to meet anyone. In the dormitory I had a room to myself, four plasterboard walls with a closet built square into the room. Going in and out, I did little more than exchange nods with the other tenants,

most of them Filipinos, small mahogany men with carefully combed hair and creased pants who looked alike to
me. On later occasions, when we talked and one mentioned that he came to California before the First World
War, I realized I could not read the physical clues to their
ages. The Filipinos were mostly bachelors. Some of them
wanted to make enough money to return home or to
bring their families to California. Others were just working and waiting.

It was from the hotel engineer, Harry Gustafson, that I
learned about the guests of the hotel. I got to talking with
him a week after I started, when I came on duty about
seven in the morning. Soon I would stop by before the
noon and evening shifts to smoke a cigaret in his office and
storeroom at the bottom between the employment office
and the cafeteria. He was as tall as I, about six feet three,
but he outweighed me by thirty-five pounds. Around his
workshop he walked heavily, nicking the tables and cabi-
nets with his work shoes. But his hands were quick and
practiced. He smoked cigarets by cupping them, causing
a deep stain on the heel of his right hand.

Harry liked to believe that not much had changed on
the island over the years and reminisced about times he
could not himself have known, which is not too different
from what Gibbon and Parkman did. The detail of what
it had been like to go to the seaside in California at the
turn of the century he probably got from the old ladies
who drank tea every afternoon on the inside patio. During the 1890s the approach to the newly built hotel was
the same as today, except that there were no shops nearby
and the mall was planted with orange and lime trees. The
grandiose blue palms were installed later. Passengers off
the ferry were met by horse-drawn carriages and luggage

vans; the porters wore leather aprons and carried canvas umbrellas, although, Harry said mysteriously, it did not rain as much in the summer in those days. Rich Californians, many of them from San Francisco and the central valley, would travel to San Diego in railroad Pullmans in early June, bringing children and pets and servants, and year after year they renewed safe acquaintanceships. During the mid-1920s, when Harry began work at the hotel, these families still came regularly, noticing but not mixing with the actors and directors and producers who drove down from Hollywood in Pierce-Arrow limousines and Stutz Black Hawks and Bearcats.

"These people have class, real rich class," Harry said one evening, "and a kid like you might learn something from them, but you can be damn sure that they won't give you anything. Rich people are stingy; they get stingy from being rich. I'm not quite sure just how that comes about."

"It's a trick of confidence, Harry," I told him. "If you expect everything, you aren't grateful for it."

Harry looked at me hard and then laughed. "A kid like you isn't going to learn. You're a wise-ass."

His opinion did not keep him from continuing accounts of the old days; and it was he who got me out of the employees' dining room only two weeks after I began work. "I talked to that greaseball, Sergio," he told me one afternoon, "and I think you can get a room-service waiter's job without a union ticket. He's having trouble holding on to waiters. Some quit to go to the tracks, Del Mar mostly."

"What if the union steward in San Diego finds out?"

"Well, I suppose Sergio will say that you lied to him, won't he?"

The headwaiter for "in service," Sergio was a nervous

Italian refugee from the war in Europe, whose rapid English was learned in the best Swiss hotels, I was told by a woman who also had fled Europe and now lived as a year-round guest in the hotel. How he reached California he never said. The room-service waiters disputed him habitually as a form of repartee. It sometimes turned vicious, as on a day when Sergio asked one of the waiters to carry his torn vanilla-colored flannel pants down to the seamstress. The waiter was outraged and went into the corridor to declare loudly that he was not about to carry pants for a Dago draft dodger. Sergio danced around him threateningly, his maroon tuxedo coat flapping over the top of his shorts, his garters stretched over his hairy calves. But he and the waiter didn't mix it up—there was too much noise, too much gesture for that. The waiter quit the same day, and it was his job I took. Sergio didn't ask about the ticket.

At the end of the next week I received a check that read: "June 19, 1941, Pay to John Sirovich the Sum of Thirty-three dollars and twenty cents, Social Security No. 521–16–1810." Now that I had more money, I checked out of the dormitory and found a place about four blocks from the hotel, off the southside piers, where there stood a few older houses with hard, permanently damp dirt instead of grass below their porches. I found the house through the want-ad section of the island daily; it was owned by a husband and wife who were letting their "front room." When I told them I would take it, after an inspection that determined little more than the availability of a bed and a bureau, the wife asked whether I was Catholic. I was not annoyed, or surprised. This I take to be allowable, for all my life I have been asked similar questions. "Is that a Russian name?" strangers ask hopefully—or else, Hungarian, Swedish, Slovakian, or, improbably, Irish or Welsh. Where I come from, your origins are fair game unless you are Jewish. I told my new landlady that I was not Catholic, and when she persisted I said I was Greek Orthodox. On hearing this, she and her husband appeared to be relieved and gratified. I should have been warned, not by their religiosity, but by their unsteadiness. At midmorning they were slightly drunk, and as I left, they stood in the doorway, short cuckoo-clock figures wearing sweaters and slippers, stiffly holding each other around the waist and smiling as they turned to go inside.

The second night, I came into my new room about midnight, after waiting tables in the hotel bar, where I worked after the dinner hour for three dollars overtime pay plus tips. Dropping my white pants and shirt in a chair, I leaned back in the bed. Just as I was letting go of time, I heard a shuffling of slippered feet, whispers, and, louder than these, a singsong voice. "A member is a limb, or part of the body . . . which is called in Scripture His body." I opened my eyes. At the foot of the bed stood the husband and wife and, between them, a boy of ten or eleven who was naked at least to the waist—I could not see below the footboard. "All the members are necessary to form one entire natural body, so are all true believers in their different places and offices."

"Our brother in Christ," the woman said to me in a voice that gargled on tears. "Our son wants to read you the Catechism of the Church of England." The boy stood motionless, holding a prayer book stiffly before him, his collarbones pushed forward from his small shoulders by the tension of this gesture.

"You're kidding," I said.

"Our brother in Christ," she repeated. "You are of the

Old Faith." She nudged the boy, who peered at me: the three figures were lighted from the doorway they had entered.

The boy resumed reading in a thin, rhythmic, but not intense voice: "But God has other sons, not *born* so, but *made* so by Baptism, for those who were naturally children of wrath, being regenerate, are made His children by adoption and grace."

When he paused I broke in: "For God's sake!" The boy's face showed expression for the first time. He frowned and was reproachful and grave. I sat up, pushing against the sheets with the heels of my palms. "I really would like to hear more," I said to the father, "but this just isn't a good time for me."

They backed away, the woman quizzical, the last to turn. Her husband put his hand on the boy's bony shoulder and they left the room ceremoniously. I fell back, agitated and ashamed. As I began to anticipate how I could move out even if I had to abandon the rest of my first week's rent, I found myself thinking of Father Oliver of St. Barnabas Church in my hometown.

Chapter

2

The Anglicans and I go back together quite a way. When I was in elementary school, my gym teacher, Miss Boswell, said to me, "John, you know, don't you, that the Orthodox share communion with us Anglicans?" I didn't know what such sharing meant, but other Anglicans were waiting for me. On my high school transcript I once saw typewritten: "John Sirovich, Orthodox (not Catholic)"; written in hand over it was the further notation "Serbian Orthodox." And when I went to the university, I put "Serbian Orthodox" down on my matriculation sheet, with the result that the local Episcopal church welcomed me to services. At the bottom of the form letter was a note: "Dear Student: As you perhaps know, there is no Orthodox church in our midst. We are proud to claim you as one of us under the rules agreed upon by the Committee of Protestant, Catholic, and Jewish Clergy that advises the Deans of Men and Women. Do please join us soon." By this time I knew the doctrinal arguments by which the Episcopalians will lay hands on homeless Orthodox. "It is not necessary that Traditions and Ceremonies be in all places one, and utterly like."

My family's last house, where my father now lives, is across the street from St. Barnabas. The buildings on this street, Father Oliver and I agreed one morning after matins, can be seen as landmarks in the social history of the city. The original plan of the city, now its business district, is a grid almost a mile square built of streets laid horizontal and perpendicular to Front Street alongside the river. After the turn of the century, a large north-south avenue called the Base Line was put down. As the grid itself is not true to the compass, the Base Line cuts its edge into a series of truncated and uneven blocks. Our block is one of these, the outer reach and the dead end of downtown. Father Oliver said it reveals at once the pretensions and limitations of American boosterism. That sounds rather grand and in any event it does not explain how you can live next to people without being their neighbors, as happens in Western cities that started late and grew fast until the Great Depression struck, leaving people hesitant but not unready, like players caught between chairs when the music stops.

On the southwest corner of our street is a three-story building of cream-colored brick put up in 1928 as a private secretarial school, which failed five years later. The property was assumed as the Business College of the local university, but the place lacks the air of collegiate leisure. The students tend not to hang around the main entrance, nor attract ice cream and tamale vendors into the street. Some of them carry leatherette briefcases, quite unlike my classmates at the state university who cradled books with one hand against the hip, like a discus.

Next to the college is the rectory of St. Barnabas. The church is red sandstone built in imitation of Durham Cathedral, with a curious interruption in its Norman structure: the unfinished front towers are lower than the roof line, whereas the central tower rises eighty feet above the floor of the crossing of the church. An empty lot owned by the parish is a buffer between St. Barnabas and the Bible Center on the corner. This building, the office for several fundamentalist Protestant churches, resembles a mean Scottish castle, with low round towers into which narrow windows are set randomly. Opposite it, on our side of the street, is a series of attached one-story apartments, each with an entrance one step up from the sidewalk. These are occupied by people who tend to be without cars or children and who you don't often see outside, sitting on the stoops at sundown. It is a conceit of mine that like their dwellings they are somehow tentative, stationery salesmen living with common-law wives or old barbers who "fill in" at the shops in the hotels.

Next to the terraces is a matched pair of solid houses built in 1910, made of what my father calls "Indiana pressed brick," which sit on a platform of soil above the sidewalk. Small plots of grass below separate the sidewalk from the street. Around ours, the second, my father fitted low, heavy steel railings, using odd lengths of pipe and joints taken from the gas company where he works. Next to our house is a parking lot whose wire fence forms a trapezoid, because here the Base Line slants across our street. The parking lot faces St. Barnabas but opens its traffic away from it. Commenting on this, Father Oliver said that most blessings are small; "but then again," he added, "most circumstances are small."

"It seems ridiculous to ask," I asked soon after we met, "but how did St. Barnabas come to be here?"

"It's not ridiculous. Poor St. Barnabas was never meant to be caught between Mammon on the right and Melanchthon on the left."

"Maybe," I said, looking at his collection of dinner bells on the refectory table, ranked to both ends from the center by their sizes, "maybe St. Barnabas should be written up as a study in local geopolitics."

"You may write it, John, for there are outward and visible signs. But I should warn you nothing is at issue. My parishioners are too affluent to live near the church nowadays, and are too few to build a second church farther from town. The fact is that they don't argue about the location any longer. The deacons might not be discouraged if they did."

"Are you discouraged?"

"I'm sure not. My expectations are never long-standing."

"Mine are," I replied.

He laughed. "How on earth can you tell at your age?"

"It seems to me that being young doesn't disqualify you from anticipating that things won't work out. Is there a particular age after which you do not expect anything personally momentous?"

"You ask the wrong man, surely. Being celibate, I hope not to be disappointed in love. Still a parish priest at forty-eight, I don't expect to become a bishop. Being an author of mystery stories and religious tracts, which some people hold to be the same thing, I certainly will not win a Pulitzer Prize."

"What of saving souls, then?"

"Well," he said, "I suppose an Anglican should consider it gross to count."

But he did count, especially as his congregation dwindled. On the rolls it numbered no more than three hundred, and at Sunday masses there were but seventy or eighty people in the pews at one time, many of them old women clutching their black missals like passports. The population of our city had not increased since the Depression, and few parishioners had moved in recently. Father Oliver, a High Anglican who subscribed to Catholic doctrine except for the Petrine Supremacy, was not in a favorable position to win converts. He could not hope to draw those Protestants who "turned" Episcopalian to gain prestige but who surely would feel they had overshot their mark were they to hear the mass at St. Barnabas and watch Father Oliver and his altar boys, of which I was one for a time, move about a dim and scented stage. Occasionally, travelers staying at the downtown hotels would attend vespers or masses, but these were usually proper American Episcopalians rather than Anglicans. Father Oliver said that you could generally recognize a Low Church layman by his compulsion to tell the pastor how much he "enjoyed" the sermon. High churchgoers are harder to please, or to instruct.

It was perhaps indicative of the lack of native vigor that I should act the votary at St. Barnabas. I was strange both to the congregation and to their profession, introduced to Father Oliver by the older of two brothers named Haddon, whose parents had come from Delaware to our city before the World War. Father Oliver said that our meeting was fortuitous less because he found a helper than because he made a friend. I was not adept on the altar. Too many times I mistook the order of the mass, or lost my place in the psalter when reading aloud, although the communicants in the pews below appeared to be undisturbed. "Help me, Lord, for there is not one Godly man left: the faithful are diminished . . . from among the children of men." "Not diminished, John," Father Oliver said. "Minished. Minished." He was, I think, resigned and not surprised; he noted that like most Orthodox, I was not an enthusiastic deist. Of course, he was right. My father regarded the Serbian Orthodox church as entirely nationalistic. I was at least twelve years old before I recognized the crucial designations in the Balkans. My father and his friends, most of them miners who came to town from the northern coal fields, would sit in the evening to recount stories of the Old Country and now and then spoke of someone as a "Turk." Gradually it occurred to me that such a person was not descended from the natives of Anatolia but, rather, was a Serbian whose family, God knows how many centuries ago, had been converted to Islam on threat of death. My father and his friends, sitting in chairs and rockers, their shoes braced against the rails of the porch overlooking the unlighted Bible Center, found it uncreditable that a man could become a Moslem and remain a Serb. They accommodated their unease by converting a man's nationality rather than admit his religion. Telling Father Oliver this, I said of my casualness in following the liturgy, "I can't excuse myself, but maybe I can explain myself."

"It amounts to the same thing in the end," he replied. He did not himself explain much and I never learned his biography sequentially. He was born in Kansas and attended Brown University in Providence, but was ordained in England. In his late thirties he arrived in our city to accept the parish of St. Barnabas, it being generally held that he suffered from consumption. One of the Haddon brothers maintained that the good priest, as he always called him, must have been found out scandalously in his preceding parish and forced to bolt. I suppose that is possible, but the source of the suggestion is tainted because this same brother wondered warily why their father, a music tutor who died when the boys were young, had left Delaware College, at Newark, where he had been a tenured professor.

Whether or not he was tubercular, Father Oliver was certainly not robust. He looked less tall than his six feet because of stooping, and he was especially thin in the forearms and shoulders. He brushed his light-blond hair straight back without a part; at the temples it looked like spun sugar. In his clerical black he seemed spent, but not so in the library of the rectory when he wore a sack suit and moved easily before the shelves that held his books and the mementos of his travels. When I reach for memory, I remember him like that, when we talked alone— from the time I met him in the late spring of my college sophomore year.

He had developed a passion for the works of the Church Fathers of the East—Gregory of Nyssa, Clement, and Basil the Great—and had written a pamphlet on the grandmother of Basil named Macrina. She was, he maintained, the true founder among the religious of the monastic regimen that renounced both worldly passions and possessions. "You know that the first monks were probably women?"

"It seems odd. I mean, odd now," I said.

"Of course. Women are subsumed by mankind." Father Oliver professed disappointment that I showed small interest in the early Church Fathers, for he pretended to the notion (disproved by his own expert attention) that these figures were comprehended best by those steeped in the Byzantine rites. Even though he had written one book and several pamphlets on the second- and third- and fourth-century Christian saints of Asia Minor, he claimed to find it hard to free himself from the syllogistic yes or no of the West.

"It is the same truth, isn't it, in the end? I mean East and West."

"Perhaps not," he said. "The Holy Wisdom is not reached by straight Roman roads. Do you know the Gnostics?"

I said, "They were never satisfied by answers?"

"You are, John, intolerant of the search for the unperceived. No, don't protest. I accept that you keenly pursue ideas. But you want them to add up."

"Like a pragmatist's grocery list?" Father Oliver laughed. "It's not mystery I don't tolerate, not really: it is the defense made for it. Mystics are excused from explaining themselves on the grounds that mysticism is inexplicable."

"But that," Father Oliver argued, "is one of the mechanisms of knowledge—not just of faith. Not everything in the universe can be described, let alone proven. The fact is that we must know some things not comprehending the fact of how we know."

"Well, saying that only proves itself. All truisms are stagy. And look both ways."

"Agreed. But we couldn't manage without paradox. Language is full of convenient contradictions. The Athanasian Creed speaks of 'coeternal,' which I admit is quite odd."

He did not press me on the early Church Fathers. Indeed, he never pressed. My visits to the rectory were actually not many and were made at my own rate. When I came to town from the university for a weekend—which was rare, because I worked for board and room throughout the term and during the short holidays—I would volunteer for altar duty by appearing at the rectory door anytime on a Saturday to ask if I was wanted. I never telephoned, maybe because using the telephone to make appointments is not common to immigrant working people, who typically will drive miles to visit friends without notice.

Other altar boys and the Sunday school "group leaders" were in the rectory at times, especially the Haddon brothers, but it seems to me that Father Oliver tried to avoid maintaining a circle of young men, even informally, except to give us a "snack tea" at the long refectory table, where we seated ourselves in order of size, like the row of bells he had collected on his travels. After saying the short prayer, we were given scones (which we didn't try to pronounce), served hot by his housekeeper, Mrs. Bradley. We layered them with butter and jam or honey taken from little pots. Attended by the particularly respectful younger boys, this ceremony was satirized by the second Haddon, whose name is Charles but who is called "Jump," as a scene that could best be played by Leslie Howard. I admit that I didn't particularly like the occasions when Father Oliver would say, after ringing one of his bells to summon stragglers from the living room, "It's teatime in Port Moresby," naming one or another exotic city where he had bought the bell then sounding.

What I did like without self-consciousness were those times we talked about his writing in his library or as we walked along the Base Line to reach the Central Library. He said that his mystery stories paid him more in royalties than the "living" he received from the parish. These were longish stories, ten thousand words or more, that appeared in *Collier's* and more often in Street and Smith magazines. He had published one novel, *The Prayer Wheel*, in which a Church of England cleric is called upon to solve a murder perpetrated inside a locked room: the victim is killed by a small but deadly Asian snake named a krait. I read a number of his mystery stories but cannot say that they convinced my interest—they were mannered and lacked the energetic style of his religious pieces. He never asked me what I thought of them.

What we tended to talk about were the principles pertinent to all writing. It was probably characteristic that I argued that a reader, at bottom, deserves to find something new. "You underrate novelty," I told him. "You may think too much on eternity, like Andrew Marvell."

"Not so! Not so! It isn't fresh information we want. It's plain problems."

"I'm not talking of philosophy."

"Neither am I. Most writing creates its own tension by means of delay: the writer knows the end; the reader waits on it."

"That's Zane Grey."

"It's also Stendhal and Hardy, who tell you of a complication, usually the undefined relation between people, and then resolve it."

Father Oliver himself never asked me questions about the undefined relation between my family and people outside. Our house was not more than sixty yards from the rectory, yet Father Oliver was never inside it, and neither my father nor my mother, during the brief period I knew Father Oliver while she was alive, sought to meet him. My father looked upon my association with St. Barnabas as transient and exotic, not unlike some of my college studies. It was accepted that I did not mix my family into the affairs of school. This sometimes puzzled my teachers and the parents of my classmates, though they didn't assume I wanted to disguise my origins, for they had too often heard me describe pridefully my mother's incredible early years and my father's surviving national inheritance. Yet they often regarded my family, like some other immigrants, as a case history that proves the grand experience of America. My mother was uninterested when as a boy I reported that my teachers thought that someone ought to "write down" her life's story.

What Father Oliver thought of my family's isolation I cannot say. It was altogether easy for us not to discuss my beginnings or his own. Maybe because of this we found it awkward to speak of the future when I said good-bye. Once the university graduation ceremonies were concluded, the last week of May, I went by the rectory. I found him at the back of the church in the atrium, as he called it, standing on the cement walk and looking at a meager garden bordered by Sierra junipers pruned narrowly to look like Italian cypresses.

"It ought to be better."

"Do you think it's the climate? High altitude and little water?"

"That's a brave explanation, John. I can scarcely keep down the Russian thistle that blows across from the parking lot. I fancied once creating a Shakespeare garden, or maybe just one for Ophelia with rosemary, pansies, fennel, columbines, and rue. But you didn't come by to listen to failed hopes, did you?"

"I'm off in a couple of days."

"Moving on. 'Then departed Barnabas to Tarsus.'"

"I think I'll go to California." He smiled. "I've heard of a place near San Diego where I can work through the summer at least, and then maybe I'll go up to San Francisco."

"And then?"

"I'm not sure."

"That sounds ominously free. But it's summer. You mean to go to Yale this fall?"

"I have a notion I ought not to make plans. That way I might not make mistakes."

"It's a nice thought, John, but I doubt the cosmos works without accidents."

"I wouldn't mind a few accidents. I can't feel the present. Since I was a boy making straight A's, people have been telling me what a great future I have."

"Time, isn't it? I suspect you cannot be really content as long as you have time ahead."

"I'm not looking for something in particular."

"It's worse, John, if you're looking for everything in particular. I pray you don't find it the worst way—in war."

"You're so sure we'll enter the war?"

"You don't accept it because here the war seems distant, but in the East it's different, as I found in New York this spring. There was a martial air." He paused. I reached down to pick up a pebble from the garden and scaled it over the junipers into the alley. "I won't keep you," Father Oliver said. "Do wait a moment." He walked to the screened back porch, off the kitchen of the rectory, and shortly reappeared carrying a package. "It's a present of no great worth, as befits a genteel clergyman."

I smiled and shook his outstretched hand, minding not to grip too hard. "I'll write you."

"No, you won't. But I'll see you again."

What I carried to California was a green leather-bound edition of Milton's *Paradise Lost* and *Paradise Regained*.

The corners of two pages were bent back and on these I found underlined in pencil:

I made him just and right,
Sufficient to have stood, though free to fall.

I formed them free, and free they must remain
Till they enthrall themselves. . . .

Chapter

3

Not even a cautionary Milton could temper my staying a lodger in a house of mad Anglicans, nor was I assured when the night visit was not repeated. On my day off, a Thursday that was the sixth day of the rent week, I put together my clothes, a dollar-twenty-five Big Ben, Father Oliver's gift, a British paperbound edition of *King John*, and a lightweight raincoat I had managed to buy on the boulevard, and went room-hunting once again. The land-lady met me in the hallway before the front door.

"Are you taking a trip, then?"

"I suppose you could say that."

"I hope you are well?"

"I'm okay. I just need a change."

"Of course. My husband and I go to Catalina for a change. It's an island, you know. Of course, with our son in school we don't go far. My husband has two older chil-dren who never come here."

"Well," I said. "Thank you."

"That's kind."

This time I looked at a section farther from the hotel, about a mile away but still on the side near the commercial wharves. After walking up and down a dozen blocks while fog drifted across the town from the northwest, leaving the air close and me unhopeful, I finally found a rooming house. It consisted of three floors, six single rooms on each of two floors over a store on the ground, the business of which was obscure to me on first impression. The room was shown by a woman of about thirty with shiny black hair and olive skin. She told me she was just helping out the owner, but she conveyed a certain authority. As I followed her to the second floor, I was stirred. She was busty and small-waisted and her legs showed strong calves. After I said I would take the room, she told me to "pay the Greek in the store later." I asked her what her name was. "Dolores," she said, "but it won't do you a bit of good." The first night in my new room, which held the heat as the sun set over the glassy bay, I felt torpid until I reached sleep; then I dreamed of Byron at Ravenna and his mistress the Countess Guiccioli. Byron said she was a trifle short from knee to heel.

The next morning I went straight to work without stopping by the store below, but returned during the afternoon break, though I had meant to invite a hotel swimming instructor to come to the public beach south of the hotel. This was a girl from Pomona College who had asked Harry several times about me. "You take it from there, sport." But I didn't ask her and I didn't go swimming. I picked up a bundle of clean work clothes from the hotel laundry, the white shirt and pants and the red Philip Morris jacket with the elastic loop holding its two wings together, and walked back to the rooming house under the high sun.

The storefront was nondescript, a door on the left, the rest finished by three lozenge-shaped panes of plate glass painted black at the top, the bottom covered by dirty curtains that hung from a brass pole. There was no sign on the window or door or on the frosted globe of the light that curved over the entrance. The place could be a barbershop or an employment agency for cleaning women or a union hall.

When I entered, I saw on the left wall a row of slot machines, the kind where a penny bounces and courses its way to the bottom, hitting or missing protruding nails until it disappears into one of several slots, all but the two in the center marked "Try Again." To the right, in front of the windows, four marble-topped tables were surrounded by drugstore chairs with wood bottoms and wire backs in the form of two hearts overlapped; next to these was a counter about four feet high made of plywood and unmatched strips of molding, the whole so eccentric in design that it only qualifiedly resembled a bar and a lunchroom counter and a soda fountain, though in fact it served as all three. There were no stools in front; behind were two large coffee urns, hot plates, cases of soda pop, a Heinz soup-maker, boxes of candy bars, Sen-Sen, snuff and chewing gum, nickel and dime punchboards, cigarets in flat racks, cake tins, a breadbox, and a cash register. There was also a double-glass-door refrigerator at least seven feet high; it held rows of Golden Bear beer and bottles of Nehi.

Here I spent a lot of my off-hours before I finally left the island, mostly in the back of the store, a step higher than the front and twice its depth. Two matched and worn Persian carpets divided this space. Centered on one was a pool table covered by a rectangle of green sailcloth and nearby were scarred high-backed stools, unpainted kitchen chairs, and a chaise longue of shiny cinnamon-colored plush. On the other carpet, the poker table and its chairs were of a different order. The table was supported by an hourglass base carved and planed from sienna-colored fruitwood. Six inches below the top and protruding no more than an inch was a gallery on which chips and glasses and ashtrays could be lodged. The table was covered by a blue baize kept carefully brushed to the perimeter. The low-backed walnut chairs with semicircular arms were polished from constant use.

This was the Greek's place, owned by a man who was Armenian, where goods were sold and services offered but not advertised or even listed. You could get a cup of soup or a toasted cheese sandwich or a beer or a slice of custard pie if someone was behind the counter, but at times there was no one to ask. A number of young men, now and then a girl, took turns behind the counter and were paid by some recondite accounting. All in all, the place was run by tacit agreement of regulars. Sometimes Dolores would sell cigarets or candy from the counter to strangers, and could then be seen in a familiar stance, hugging herself at the waist and staring out the window, but she drew a line on her services and if she took a beer from the icebox or poured coffee it was only for herself or the Greek. The pool table was probably in playing condition, though I never saw its surface, whereas during my time the card table was occupied off and on from eleven in the morning until midnight. Within two weeks I was at ease there, playing poker, talking to the Greek about philosophy, for which he had a renewable interest but not much reference, watching Dolores, drinking Orange Crush, trading idle remarks with others. I didn't do this right off, because I was working long hours breaking in as a room-service waiter.

As the most junior waiter, I was at the beginning under-privileged out of custom and from lack of canniness. At first I didn't recognize and anticipate the big tippers. Mainly you had to know the habits of the guests, both the "permanents" and the "new arrivals." The hotel rented a number of double rooms and small suites for the whole summer to "permanents," typically old couples who had returned to the hotel alone after all the years when their children had stayed with them on school holidays. But there were some first-time "permanents" as well, like the pair of sisters on the fourth-floor oceanfront who fled Germany in 1939. After staying for a short period with their nephew in Hollywood, they were installed by him in the hotel, "near enough," they told me, "to be watched but not seen." They were like desert birds, with sinewy arms and legs; their narrow faces were deeply browned by the California sun. They did not talk about Europe and were already at ease in the American idiom. Their nephew, a movie producer who lived in Beverly Hills, was named Sanders. "Isn't it odd," one of them said to me one morn-ing, "that we can be Jewish but our sister's son is not?" The sisters were tight tippers. For breakfast they always ordered popovers and coffee; and I would carry a forty-pound steel box with two shelves and a door, its Sterno cup lighted to keep the popovers from turning cold and brittle, all the way up to the fourth floor. For that I got a dime tip. The more experienced waiters managed not to be free when the sisters' room number was flashed on the call board. I kept them even after I learned to draw better numbers.

You could find out about arriving guests by bribing one of the desk clerks: five dollars every two weeks would buy you reliable though not exclusive information. You could also keep an eye on the florist shop, where large bouquets and fruit baskets were made ready for presentation by the management to notable new guests, though bringing a bouquet up to a room right after a guest checked in was no way to get a large tip: waiters resigned that ceremony to the bellhops. The Hollywood people, except for most of the English, were reliably generous and sometimes reckless. Among the room-service waiters there were legends of profligacy. Warner Baxter tipped one waiter fifty dollars late at night when he sent him back for another brand of soda water. The comedienne Louise Fazenda tipped twenty dollars when she took tea one afternoon on the inside patio with Jinx Falkenburg, who was playing in a tennis tournament at the hotel with her younger brother. Some of this good news was true, but it was hard to tell because such stories were designed obviously to enhance the teller.

"Harry," I told him one afternoon when I brought him a Monte Cristo cigar left on a tray from my last order of the luncheon, fresh in its ridged paper tube, "I've figured out why room-service waiters are dumb but feel privileged."

"That's no trick, John. Hell, they're like anybody with lots of time and not much to do. Touts at the track."

"That may be, but they are corrupted by being close to the rich and the famous."

"Don't you want to become rich and famous?"

"No, I'm serious. Room-service waiters see those people so closely—in their bedrooms, really—they try to imitate them. Some become snobs without money. The worst kind."

"I'm not sure that a snob with money is any better. It's funny you don't mention nooky. Don't those guys tell stories of screwing the movie stars?"

"Oh, that," I said. "Sure, phony as it is."

"Listen, kid, it may not be so phony. Stay out of the beds when you go calling with your heater. A good-looking guy like you can be an old man by the time you're twenty-two."

Once I had gained my share of the good-paying permanents, including the precise and witty eighty-year-old widow of a treasurer of the Santa Fe Railroad, and had caught new arrivals in the first flush of establishing their status at the hotel, I made a fair amount of money. My pay was thirty-five dollars a week, less Social Security; board was free; the tips from room service, breakfast, lunch, and dinner added up to fifteen dollars on an average day, or more when I drew a couple of winners. And of course I was eating prime fare, not in the employees' dining room, where I had begun work scarcely a month before, but in various safe places around the hotel: a large supply closet in the main service corridor, alcoves at the end of the corridors overlooking the inside patio, and Harry's storeroom. I cannot believe that the chef or Sergio did not know the game, which consisted of a room-service waiter's returning to the checker, especially at a time when the meal was at its height, to say that the original order had been incorrectly noted and a different entrée was needed. You then got a new entrée from the steam tables—filet mignon, sweetbreads, or squab, something expensive that could be eaten fast in one of the safe places. You risked having the second entrée billed to the guest whose complaint you had feigned, but this was a good bet if his order had been diverse—drinks, appetizers, desserts, after-dinner liqueurs—and if he appeared undemanding. Or you went another way and took your chances on the checker, arguing that the guest was sore about bad service and had kept the original entrée while waiting for a replacement. Like all bureaucratic petty crime, this was a complicated racket in which the thrill of concealment was greater than the prize. Not that much was gained in any event. Some of the older waiters developed ulcers.

Still more money came my way when Sergio, whose in-service domain included the children's dining room, asked if I'd be willing to work there for an hour before the regular lunch and dinner shifts. Another waiter had gone off to work at the tracks. I accepted only partly for the money. I was restless, and as it was I spent time-off hours at the hotel with not much to do except to swim at South Beach or play gin rummy with Harry in the storeroom.

The children's dining room was the sole public room that opened onto the inside patio: through its big bow windows the mothers and the fathers could be seen as they passed from the pool or tennis courts through the patio to their rooms at noon, or as they headed outward to the cocktail lounge about six. On the perimeter were tables with chairs for two and four and at the center tables for five and eight, these reserved for occasions when parents joined their children. Otherwise, the kids sat together or ate under the supervision of their nannies.

I drew three tables for lunch and dinner, always the same ones, and managed to get through one sitting before going on room-service duty. At one table sat an English nanny and a boy of about seven who was grossly fat. He habitually unbuttoned his waistband while eating, and at the end of the meal would sometimes rise and discover his pants falling around his ankles. The nanny was disgusted by him. She would look away when he asked for a second order of prime ribs, his favorite, and frequently said through pursed lips, "For goodness' sake, John!" when calling me to pick up a dropped fork, fetch a fresh napkin, and, most urgently, to shinny his pants back over his dimpled knees to be refastened at his distended waist. Each meal began gravely, with the nanny moving the silverware ever so slightly with her bony fingers, as if it required her final tuning, and with the boy looking anxious but sitting quite still, not tempting misfortune. The boy was at moments stolid but hardly uncurious. When I told him I had ridden the rods to California, in answer to his pestering me why I did not own an automobile, he became concerned to know all the details—where you placed your feet under the freight car, whether you could sleep and ride at the same time, whether there were any boys hitching rides on trains. The nanny looked away during such dialogs, uninterested in my low-down adventures and in the unseemly fascination they held for him. I knew the boy as Arthur, the nanny as Miss Starrett, and for some reason never heard his last name.

No more than ten days after I undertook to work the extra hours, I was summoned by Arthur's mother. One afternoon a bellhop came to the room-service waiters' call room at the end of luncheon to say a lady on the patio was asking for Big John. A waiter called Shosh was quick off the mark. He was an off-and-on actor who went from waiting tables to spend a few weeks at the Pasadena Playhouse or at summer stock theaters in Rockies resort towns as far north as Calgary. "I'll go," he said briskly and headed for the door. I held my forearm stiffly against his chest. "Look at this," said an older waiter. "Shosh is about to become a character actor. Big John is going to give him an interesting face." Shosh laughed.

The patio was free from the effects of jigsaw artistry that elsewhere gave the hotel its turrets and galleries and flower boxes and even buttresses. The patio was a hexagon framed by five tiers of corridors; over the banisters you could look down on the patio's slate floor, where trees stood in white cement pots and tables were shaded in the forenoon and early afternoon by mustard-yellow parasols that from above were like poker chips. Later, when I thought about the times I had carried trays and heaters along the corridors, I recalled that from their vantage the trees looked like a cat's cradle, but that was only after I had seen bonsai trees in Hollywood. It was at a patio table that I greeted Arthur's mother.

"Are you Big John? Of course you are. Arthur describes you vividly. You're a hero to him, as you must know. He wants to ride the rails like Big John."

"Miss Starrett will never let him."

"Ah, dear. Miss Starrett." She sighed, then patted the white pleated skirt of her dress and moved the rounded leather tie at her waist. "Do you mind sitting? I shall catch a crick in my neck."

As I sat down I recognized her almond-shaped eyes and beautifully wide mouth. She was an English actress who must have been in Hollywood a decade, since the days of the first talkies. She was now established as a popular second lead, usually the unreasonable wife of the hero or the patient friend of the hero who has an unreasonable wife.

"I hope you like Arthur. It's so important to him that you do."

"Sure, I like Arthur." That didn't sound convincing, so I added quickly, "But then, I don't see that much of him."

"That's his burden. His father and I don't spend enough

35

time with him, which accounts for Miss Starrett. No, there's no accounting for Miss Starrett." We both laughed, but oddly a long pause followed. "His father and I both travel a good deal; and we are divorced without either being remarried. Arthur goes to school in Brentwood. I'll be coming down here to take him back in mid-August."

"That's good."

"Why do you say that?"

"I don't know. I suppose I think he's pretty bored here, though there are some kids around the hotel, and swimming and the tennis classes and all that."

"He's more than just bored." She looked at me earnestly, as if to judge the effect of what she said next. "He's an ungainly, bright, affectionate, unhappy child." She came down on each adjective separately, but with her practiced diction she managed to make them mount to a conclusion.

I said, "I don't know about that, but I'll be talking with Arthur as long as I stay in the children's dining room." This was an attempt to be hopeful, but not perceiving the drift of the conversation, I managed fatuously to sound like a filling-station attendant assuring someone he'd check the plugs.

She smiled brilliantly, as if to confirm that I had said precisely the right thing. "Do you work here all year round?"

"No. I've just graduated from college and I stopped here for the summer."

"And then?"

"Well, I don't know." I smiled. "I'm trying not to have a future."

"That's refreshing. I spend far too much time listening to young actors talk about their futures."

"And what about the older ones?"

She clapped her hands below her chin and said delightedly, "They have your problem." Then we both fell silent again until she said, too hurriedly, "Could I persuade you to come to Los Angeles to tutor Arthur after he goes to school?"

"Tutor him in what?"

"I'd leave that to you—and to him."

"What about Miss Starrett?"

"She wouldn't be concerned."

"She hates him."

"That's too strong, surely."

"It's not a matter of degree. How much do you have to hate someone to be bad for them?"

She looked away to the nearby tree. Its leaves changed from the effect of the light: on the patio there was no breeze. "That's cynical. You sound as if someone had jilted you."

"We're talking about Arthur."

"Yes, of course."

"I'm not sure I'll be here after August. That's almost two months away."

"Don't decide now. Please think it over. Here, you can write me." She took from her bag a pad with a stitched leather binding, snapped out a page from the perforated top, and wrote the address. Before giving it to me, her hand hovered over the bag, then she reached in and folded two twenty-dollar bills around the notepaper and held it across the table. I slipped out one twenty and put it on the table in front of her, and put the other twenty with the address in my shirt pocket.

Chapter

4

July came. For more than a week the days began
and stayed hot as the westerly breeze failed, leaving
the island so warm that at dusk I felt quirky and expectant. When it was like that and if I was off duty, I
would walk the mile or so eastward on the boulevard
to the library, passing the women's stores and the soda
shops and luncheonettes where the jukeboxes seemed
to play all summer long Tommy Dorsey's "I'll Never
Smile Again." A few blocks past the big curve there
were duplexes, two-family attached houses, and small
apartment houses faced in cream stucco. At this hour
people sat on the cement steps, forearms on knees, listening to H. V. Kaltenborn tell the war news as they
watched the automobiles roll by and passengers alight
from streetcars on the mall. Farther eastward was a
church and a convent school, and across the boulevard
from these on the north side was a wide plot of greenery on which stood the Carnegie Library.

The library was a splendid building, not unique (as I
know from other Carnegie libraries in other towns) but
here nicely set next to a bowling green, a small Roman

temple, with bas-relief pillars formed by an extra thickness of stone. Under the flat copper roof, there was engraved on the pale marble of the frieze on the front and sides of the building: *Plato—Aristotle—Virgil—Dante—Erasmus—Shakespeare—Harvey—Milton—Pascal—Locke—Goethe—Emerson—Mill—Tennyson.* Below Shakespeare and Harvey, studded bronze doors stood open from their own weight. In early evening, walking up the steps I could hear the muted click of wooden balls on the English bowling green. The grass on the green, cut short and rolled evenly, was dusty blue in the failing light. Alongside, the library entrance shone orange. One evening I took the girl from Pomona on a walk to the library. We sat on the grass, near the bushes at the side of the building where the wisteria blossoms hung like grapes. I remember that she sat with her arms stretched straight ahead, hands clasped at her ankles, her cheek resting on a knee. We heard the rise and fall of the voices of the spectators on the far side of the green and we watched the bowlers, old men wearing straw hats, until it was thickly dark.

The girl was Elizabeth Petrie, twenty years old, born and raised in Santa Maria. Some nights we went swimming at South Beach, usually with others from the hotel: a barman who was a junior at UCLA and his girl friend, who lived year round on the island and who, when asked what she did, answered with a straight face that she was a paleontologist; and Shosh, who had taken up with Elizabeth's partner (also a junior from Pomona) in the swimming classes, a quiet girl who found it easier to fend off Shosh than he claimed. On the beach we would make small bonfires out of the slats of bottle boxes and across the sputtering light we talked randomly of fraternities and sororities and sports, and of travel, though nobody had been east of St. Louis. The war in Europe was rarely mentioned. Hollywood was itself a subject more than movies. My easy recollection of movie titles and casts of actors seemed to them eccentric, akin to bookishness. When somebody said that seals were supposed to come ashore on the spit of land where we swam, I said that, sure, the seals were mentioned in the book *I Cover the Waterfront*, though not in the movie that starred Claudette Colbert and Ben Lyons. But nobody else had seen the movie.

The water was chill by ten o'clock at night and the waves weren't much good after evening tide; yet we could ride the falling edge of the waves when swimming in to shore. I didn't get the chance to try surfing, because nobody on these night outings ever happened to bring a board. Elizabeth was a powerful swimmer and kept her head low as she turned back and forth to gasp air over the foam. In sprints on the sand she could keep up with me for twenty yards or so. Like most California girls, she was taller, stronger, and somehow cleaner than the girls I knew at home. I told Shosh that California girls might be part of an American experiment to create a master race and that they had great genes. "Yeah," he agreed, "and great tits."

The swimming was good, and so was hacking around the beach and eating late, but the talk made me feel awkward at times during the presumably serious discussions. Elizabeth accused me of being "superior," which I told her was not a crime in any event, and when she asked what it was then, I said it was the result of college class struggle. She was not inclined, when I talked that way, to give herself to the kissing and nuzzling and groping that were standard for couples whose company had persisted to a second or third date. Whether or not we would have proceeded to a senior relationship—this is what the barman from UCLA called his sleeping with the girl paleontologist—I didn't have the chance to find out. Suddenly, Elizabeth had to leave. Her father had undergone a stomach operation, requiring her to return to Santa Maria to help her mother run the drugstore they owned. I rode with her in a cab to the ferry one morning.

"Will you be back?" I asked, even though she'd earlier told me her father might not work for two or three months, according to a Dr. Stalweather, who had delivered her twenty years before and had since severed her tonsils and set a broken arm.

"Not until fall, I guess. I hope I can get to Pomona, even." We looked at the bay, where white rills formed and died fast as the ferry approached the dock. She gave me her address, which she'd already written out and took from her flat beaded purse. "Will you be near Pomona in the fall?"

I didn't answer directly. "I'll call you. I will," I said. When I said it she looked hurt. As the ferry stuttered in the slip, I inspected it closely, and when I turned back to her, she kissed me hard. I felt proud and abashed. She lifted her small suitcase and walked onto the car ramp and turned to stare at me. I watched the ferry until it was halfway across the bay, then caught the streetcar.

After Elizabeth left I began to spend more and more time at the Greek's place, first only at night—after quitting the dinner shift or about midnight if I happened to work the cocktail lounge after dinner—but sometimes I would drop in between meals. Besides Shosh, I knew only four or five regulars at the place, including a tall, wiry guy named Jackson, who had gone to Oregon State for a couple of years and now worked on and off at the airfield on Cameron Island, directly north and connected by a causeway to the island. Jackson had played varsity basketball at Corvallis and he was fast and mean. We first met in the city recreation park, playing a few games of two-man basketball and handball on the cement courts. I don't remember winning more than one game from him. At the Greek's he would sit about with the untired ease of an athlete and try to entice someone into playing gin or, failing that, matching quarters or betting the point spread on the following day's major-league baseball games. If he found no takers and was left to himself, he would sometimes hunch over the counter like a question mark, his head lowered, one leg wound around the other. Jackson played poker rarely, Shosh not at all. Shosh said that its slow action tended to ruin his fine edge with women. He was usually broke.

The Greek was to be found—except when he was in the apartment at the back of the raised platform, where only Dolores saw him—at the poker table or else seated in one of the black-lacquered captain's chairs placed every afternoon under an olive tree between the sidewalk and the street. It was commonly believed the Greek planted the olive tree years before, but there were matching trees on the same street. I could have told him that it was in a grove of olive trees that Plato started his school by talking to a subject, more or less as we did some afternoons. But I didn't.

He regularly emerged from his apartment about eleven, sat down at the poker table to talk or play, but never both, until about two o'clock, when he would put on his Panama hat and walk over to the boulevard to visit one of the two local banks and stop by a fruit stand run by another Armenian. At six he ate dinner alone at one of the marble-topped tables by the window, his back to the door. His meal was brought to him by Dolores, who cooked it in the apartment. By eight o'clock he was at the poker table, playing or watching. On Sunday afternoon he drove to the ferry in his 1933 Chrysler Imperial Eight, with its silver spokes and spare tires notched into the flat low curves of the fenders. Dolores would sit inside wearing a purple silk print dress, an Empress Eugénie hat pinned to her rich hair.

The Greek was named Tamourian, born in Bitlis, and he arrived in America in 1923 as a refugee from the Turks after they burned Smyrna. When I met him he was about forty-five, of medium height, heavy in the shoulders and solidly round at the waist. His hair was dyed entirely black; his nails were manicured and the index fingers on both hands bore heavy gold rings with square diamonds. The Greek's clothes were expensive and dated, running to white silk shirts and gray striped trousers.

At the Greek's place, other than Shosh and Jackson, the regulars I came to know best were a girl from my hometown, Nita, and her boyfriend, Spider. The girl was a Slovak from the north side of the city. She had been sixteen and in her junior year of high school when one day she left her family and took a bus to Los Angeles. How long she stayed I don't know, but she told me she worked downtown in a hotel coffee shop and later for a job printer in Alhambra. She went back home to work as a carton checker in the local brewery, met Spider, and took him back with her to California, where they now lived together in a room on the floor above mine at the Greek's place. Nita was nineteen, Spider a year younger. Together, they seemed older, because she was protective but undemonstrative. They did not hold hands even at the movies.

Spider was not much taller than Nita, five feet five or so, and he may have come by his name because he stood in a tensed, angular way. I found out from Nita that Spider's family lived on a farm along the South Platte in Nebraska, although his father and one of his brothers drove forty miles each day in a Model A to work at a small oil refinery. They had left Oklahoma when the dust storms were bad in 1931 and after fighting the drought they settled on land in Nebraska almost as dry.

Spider met Nita at a street festival on the north side, where every year during religious holidays the Slovaks and Poles who live there carry into the streets their effigies and banners held by poles trailing gold-colored ropes and tassels. They march from St. Nicholas's Catholic Church to a little square at the end of the viaduct that crosses over the railroad tracks and the riverbed to the downtown grid. After speeches are delivered, they march back. Passers-by must regard this ceremony, I've often thought, as being altogether unconnected as it moves along streets named Rycroft and Shoshone and Tennyson and Cheyenne.

When Spider met Nita, they left the same day for California. Now Spider was driving a laundry van and Nita, already experienced, worked at a small print shop on the boulevard. Spider did not talk much and he rarely looked directly at people, even those who stood near him. This was shyness but also a kind of nice unobtrusiveness. Spider felt, I came to recognize, that the affairs mentioned by strangers or spoken of on the radio had nothing to do with him. He was raised dirt poor, unschooled; for him, the world must have seemed to hold forth messages and missions only for others.

"You're an anarchist, Spider," I told him one afternoon as we stood dropping pennies at the slot machines.

"What's that?"

"Somebody who wants nothing to do with government."

"Yes, that's me." He grinned. "But that don't mean the government won't have nothin' from me."

"Well, being an anarchist is only part-time work. Spider, do you want anything?"

"What you mean?"

"I mean, do you want to own anything, or go someplace?"

"I'd like Nita to get what she wants."

"What's that?"

"I dunno."

"What about you?"

He looked distracted. Then he said, "I sure would be proud to own a Harley motorcycle. Or an Indian."

"How much does one cost?"

"One hunder eighty new."

"I hope you can. Save your money. Stay away from these damn machines."

"You like Spider, don't you?" Nita asked me as she joined me walking on her way to the print shop.

"I like him a lot."

"He says that you know everything. What a terrible disease!"

"There's no cure for it."

If Nita was usually quick to quip, smiling at discovered joys, she could be critical. Her signal was to ask questions. "How come that you let the Greek do all the talking when he gets to telling everybody how things are?"

"Promise you won't tell?"

"Sure. Unless it's funny."

"Because the Greek knows the odds at poker, he thinks he can weigh everything else. One thing has nothing to do with the other. Plato probably lost his racing bets."

"You don't argue with him."

"What's the point? He knows not to stay in for an inside straight. And he doesn't pay taxes. For him, that's enough."

Nita said, her head thrown back as she looked seriously at me, "The Greek is a pain in the ass when he gets to talking outside under that tree. You notice that Dolores never goes out there? She knows better."

"I don't know what Dolores knows. But I'd like to find out someday."

"Wow. Better watch it, Big Johnny." She strummed her fingers from a wrist held limply. "What you need is a girl. What happened to that swimmer?"

"She went home. Her father's sick."

"Shosh says that a movie actress wants you to come live with her."

"Shosh is full of it."

"But you still need a girl. It's got to be a kicker, a handsome guy like you going to the movies with Spider and me alone."

Nita was right about my not taking on the Greek. We kept a truce of sorts. The Greek told me about cards and gamblers, which I liked hearing partly because all the Serbians I knew were inveterate and colorful gamblers; and in turn I provided the Greek with an informed but uncontesting listener under the olive tree. We felt no affinity by reason of my coming from an immigrant family. As an Armenian, he was convinced that the only person worse than a Russian is a Turk. He was in fact antagonistic to Greeks, even though at times the Greeks and the Armenians were alike mistreated by the Ottomans. He liked Jews and refuted especially the truism that they are born sharp traders.

"How come you are not Orthodox?" I asked when he told me his parents had been Presbyterians.

"What the hell kind of question is that?" he said. "How come you are not Armenian?"

He liked to say that the Armenians are the only people, other than the Jews, who had once a country of their own and lost it but who still know proudly who they are. Just think of it, he would exclaim with wonderment but without regret: the Armenians never had customs inspectors, tax collectors, government clerks, census takers. He liked to speculate on what would have happened had the Armenians become a charge of the Americans, as President Wilson had proposed to the Senate. He was boastful of those countrymen (except those in Russia) who were publicly known, like the young writer William Saroyan. I told him that another writer, Michael Arlen, was an Armenian, and he believed it until he read *The Green Hat*, which Dolores brought from the Carnegie Library.

The Greek held that since Fate was implacable you could do little else in the conduct of days except be watchful. Mainly this meant not getting involved with other people. "I never had a partner. A Jewish jeweler I met in New York told me, 'Listen, don't take on another man's troubles; buy his goods, but don't buy his story.' And he was right. You got a partner, maybe his wife wants him to buy a new house; then he complains to you he needs cash, and maybe you have to sell your stake too early and you lose. Marriage, the same thing. In the Old Country you knew the woman brought a little money and furniture with her, but the big thing was she wouldn't ask you for something, or make you go someplace. Here it's bad. You know that women own the property in this country? It's a fact. They took it away from men. Wives can kill your chances, like a partner in business. I never got married in this country. I don't make bad bets."

The Greek now and again would stick my attention. He had a talent for analogy that surprised me. Had he known of my surprise, I suppose that as a betting man he would have said that if you hold a large number of observations you will inevitably once in a while put together a good hand. He was intolerant of formal education and scorned "Joe Colleges who don't have two dimes to rub together," comparing them to men he knew who got rich by the exercise of their native wit—an Armenian wholesale grocer in Fresno and a Dalmatian who owned a fleet of tuna boats out of San Pedro. One day as I sat with the Greek and a friend of his, a man in his sixties who ran a garage on the spit and who came by twice a week to sit at long poker sessions, the Greek suddenly asked me about my physiognomy. "Dolores says that you look like an American."

"Who else would I look like? I am an American."

"I know you are. You're two hundred percent American. I'll bet you don't look like your mother or father. I seen it a hundred times. Everybody looks American right off."

"Listen," I told him, "you are talking about the way people act, not how they look. After all, we all go to the same schools."

"I never went to school here," the Greek said. "And I

never went much to school in the Old Country, neither. But the Americans know what they are doing. Everybody has to go to school in this country. If you don't go, they come get you, just like the army; and by the time they come out they are all alike. My friend Hakob in Fresno, he's got three sons and two daughters, and all of them are just as American as Henry Ford. That's the way it goes here. You remember we was talking once about the Turks, about how they took the young boys away from the other people—like your people, the Serbians—and raised them to be the strongest and meanest Turks. What was it they called them?"

"Janissaries," I told him.

"That's right. Maybe you're one of them Janissaries. What happened is that the Americans took you into their schools and made you the most American. If you end up with money, you'll say it's because the system here made it happen. That's not so, but you'll believe it. And if you're rich enough, you'll make other people believe it."

I was scornful, but that night as I lay in my room stripped down to my skin because of the July heat, I let stray into the back rooms of my mind the notion that I was somehow enlisted. I did not resent it. I suppose I felt a loyalty to the future.

Chapter

5

Although my days were nearly alike, schedules repeated, I did not concede to routine. I made things harder by beginning and tracing familiar events anew. Why did I do this? Not from boredom, I am quite certain, nor from fancy. I would wake up about seven o'clock, sweating in the sheets, go down the hall to the shower, return to put on white shirt and socks and pants, black shoes and stretch belt, and stuff into my pocket the Ready Fix bow tie and loop the red monkey jacket inside my elbow. Downstairs I stopped by to drink a cup of coffee. If Nita was around she would fry me three or four eggs with cayenne pepper, but usually I didn't eat. Sometimes Dolores came out of the apartment at the back to have a cup with me, standing behind the counter, a knitted sweater thrown over her rounded shoulders, hands clasped at her waist, a cigaret held straight between her bowed lips. She did not pour my coffee even when we were alone, nor would she acknowledge that I looked at her pleasurably in the early light. Now and then she smiled, as if distracted by admiration, the Gioconda smile.

About seven-thirty I would walk the eight blocks to the

hotel, approaching from the south, where the salt air was lightly acrid. I would manage another cup of coffee before taking my first number of the day. From eight to ten o'clock it was heavy traffic in the kitchen, where the second chef supervised three women at the steam tables and coffee urns, a couple of fry cooks, a butcher—and the assistant pastry chef, who opened the kitchen at six to roll dough. The big chef didn't concern himself with breakfast and arrived about ten, just after the main pastry chef and the salad-makers and the butchers and the vegetable cooks appeared.

By ten-thirty I was usually free, but only for an hour and a half. If I felt sleepy from having stayed up late playing cards at the Greek's or from taking in a ten-o'clock movie in San Diego, I could lie down in Harry's office on a cot he kept so he could spend the night when he for some reason did not go home to the small bungalow where he lived with his wife and two young daughters. Otherwise, I would carry my trunks down to South Beach to swim with Shosh, a few of the main dining-room waiters, and a law student from USC, who handled the rentals of sailboats at the hotel's bayside pier. One or two mornings a week Nita would come over to join us on the beach. If there were six or seven of us gathered, the USC guy would produce a volleyball and net, to the especial delight of Nita, who when sides were drawn danced and cheered as if her dowry were at stake. The shortest one of us on the beach, Nita played a spirited backcourt, her black eyes and wide mouth moving excitedly as she darted forward to boost the ball before it hit the sand. Later, she told me those were the happiest hours of her life. I believe it.

Other days, if I came off breakfast late, eleven-thirty or so, there was only a short time before I had to take numbers from the board for luncheon. Even so, I stayed out of the call room to avoid the bull sessions held there by three or four of the regulars, the older waiters who had worked summer and winter at the hotel for many years and the other waiters, who like swallows moved up and down the West Coast seasonally but whose opinions were not for that different. The talk always ended, however introduced, with money and sex and famous people. Politics did not intrude except as personalities could be condemned. Franklin D. Roosevelt and his wife were good for comment at least once a day, and only slightly less often, Hitler and Churchill. Charles A. Lindbergh's fight against American involvement in the European war could ignite a discussion, but the issue was usually the state of his popularity rather than his politics. Salacious asides were delivered on the true cause of Jean Harlow's death, the lust of movie producers, the drinking of the young actress Frances Farmer. Arguments rose over numbers: the total count of divorces in the Roosevelt family, Louis B. Mayer's salary, the frequency of Charlie Chaplin's marriages, how many days Aimee Semple McPherson spent in the desert. These arguments were never settled, and if appealed to a third person, his verdict was immediately rejected. Once or twice someone suggested that I be consulted, but other disputants held that a college education does not qualify one to verify facts, there being in their minds, quite rightly, a distinction between data and systematic knowledge.

Sometimes, when the weather fell limp from the wet northerly wind, I stayed in the main kitchen to drink coffee and read the Los Angeles papers. This was especially congenial the half hour before dinner and during a lull about ten o'clock which was the denouement of the day.

The main kitchen was entirely open except for the thick columns that supported cross vaults; the ceiling honeycomb trapped the noises of crockery and metal and the voices of the cooking crew and the captains, waiters, busboys, and cleaners. Out of their way but in view, I staked out a bench between the pastry chef's gas-fired ovens and the steam tables. I am now, a long time after, not inclined to accept accidents of place and the coincidence of time as being disinterested. Even had I not claimed the bench, I probably would have come to know the pastry chef. But would I have found the girl who in the end caused me to leave the island?

The pastry chef was born on the Don. His name was Leonid Novoroshoff. He found me out as a fellow Slav and immediately narrated his story. I was not surprised by his candor, though later I warned him against it. Americans and Russians may be alike in their eagerness to tell their life stories, living as they do in nearly empty spaces, but Leonid doubted my explanation. He knew few Americans well, having stayed mostly with Russians in the West Coast towns where he'd worked, Seattle and San Francisco and Los Angeles and Sacramento. I was surprised when he told me he knew Czech better than English. He had been attached to a company of Czech soldiers that fled eastward along the Trans-Siberian Railway in the White Russian army under the command of Admiral Kolchak.

Together we of course spoke English, but when others were around he would intersperse his remarks to me with a kind of basic Slavic that relies on personal pronouns and simple nouns. He did this in part out of revenge, especially when we were near those waiters who complained they couldn't understand his accent. Leonid was frequently excited, but never more so than when I once persisted in a relentless but, as it proved, aimless desire to clear up the facts at hand. His fear heightened, probably, because there was no issue.

"Were you in Vladivostok when Kolchak lost, then?"

"Yes."

"And how did you get to America?"

"I got here. I took a boat."

"Of course, but did you leave from Vladivostok, or from somewhere else?"

"What do you mean?"

"Well," I said, pressing, "didn't some of the people with Kolchak go south into China?"

"I don't know."

"But you did leave Siberia. When was that?"

"After the war."

"How come the local soviet in Siberia let you go?"

He turned aside, his back to me behind the serving counter, his feet skittish. "Why do you ask, Johnny? It's a million miles."

I said, surprising myself, "You came on an American troop boat."

"Yes, troops. You know about that?"

"A friend of my father got his citizenship by joining the American Army and going to fight the Reds in Siberia."

Leonid looked from side to side. I was moved by uncertainty now that I had tripped into his secret. "It's very bad, you see."

"I won't say anything. But you have got to change your story, Leon. Forget about Kolchak and Vladivostok most of all. Why not just say you came here from Europe."

"I don't understand."

"Why mention Siberia? Why not just be a regular immigrant like millions of Slavs? This country is full of people who aren't quite sure where they landed. My mother thought she came into New York and found out twenty years later that she landed in Baltimore."

"Big John, I told you because you want to know. There is a Russian saying: You make a friend, you make a secret. Is that the right way to say?"

"I guess so. But listen, the thing is not how you make secrets but how you keep them. Every time somebody asks me if I can keep a secret, I can't help noticing he's just about to break one." I had begun this talk as a prosecutor with no case and ended as a judge with no authority, but there was no helping it now.

The next morning he caught my sleeve as I passed into the corridor from the kitchen and circled me, drawing me to the wall. "You really won't say nothing?"

"I told you not."

"It's bad for me. They send me back to Russia if they find me."

"No, Leon, they won't. Americans aren't sending people back to Russia. It would be giving them troops."

"But you be careful?"

"I will. I don't know what to say now, Leonid. I can only tell you that I trust myself."

"I wish you fought with me. Good men." His eyes widened: he was unburdened but safe, a man relieved.

I made a secret with the girl, too, but unlike Leonid's, it had no reference to my own past and no effect on it. I remember the girl only for herself. I saw her from a distance the first day I came into the kitchen and afterward

I would look at the steam tables in hope of catching a view of her leaning against the counter, her hard round breasts showing against her blouse. She was no more than twenty, a tall, strong girl whose skin flushed to an orange color because of the heat rising from the tables and whose blond hair drew up into ringlets on her forehead. She was not herself confident and seemed unaware of her body. She filled her clothing as she moved and I watched the outlines of her thighs and the cleavage of her young back. When I began to hang out in the kitchen reading the morning and, later, the stock and racing editions, I discovered myself glancing at her clandestinely. Out of a sense of discipline, as if it were healthful, I tried to ration the times I looked at her directly. Usually I failed. Even so, I knew more about her husband than about her.

He was one of the three hotel butchers, a man of thirty-five named George Fancher, who was a rarity on the staff for having been born on the island of parents who themselves were employed at the hotel, his mother the assistant housekeeper and his father a boilerman who worked for Harry. George and his wife lived with his parents on the coast road toward the Mexican border. Other than that, I knew him only from appearances. Because he was often in and out of the walk-in cooler, he wore a straw hat with the brim cut back to the band, so that it stressed his heavy neck muscles; and under his white butcher's coat his T-shirt was cut off at the shoulder seams to show his biceps. Fancher was obviously pleased by his young wife and seemed to confirm this by offhandedly not speaking to her, although in the kitchen they were not more than twenty yards apart. She acknowledged his assurance by being careful not to reply to waiters and busboys, who never gave up attempts to make her talk to them as they admired her figure when she turned quickly or leaned forward over the steam tables. She didn't talk to me either until I caught her outside the hotel one afternoon. Then she had no choice, whatever was her resolve.

She stood at the streetcar stop at the curve in the boulevard, just opposite the small office building that held the print shop alongside its street entrance. When she boarded the car and I followed her on the run, I saw Nita looking out from the shopwindow. She grinned and swept her hands low across her waist, giving me the baseball umpire's "safe" sign as I caught the handrail on the car's open back door.

"What's your name?" I asked as I sat down next to her on the rattan seat.

"You know."

"No," I said, lying. "I know your husband's name."

"It's Jean."

"Great. I'm John."

"I know. Leon talks about you all the time. Do you know Russian, really?"

"Not really. I'm as American as can be, which is going pretty far."

Tilting her head, she looked at me curiously. Up close I saw how blond her hair was, white almost, especially fine where it laced a delicate ladder down the column of her neck.

"Where are you going?" Jean asked gravely.

"The streetcar only goes to the ferry."

"You know what I mean. Are you going to San Diego?"

"Jean, I'm following you."

"Oh. That's a compliment, I know, but it isn't right. I mean that my husband, George, he won't like anything like that."

I took her by the arm just then, seeing the library stop a block ahead, and pulled the twill rope overhead. I took her arm, urging her to the exit. After a moment's hesitation, she stepped to the accordion doors and jumped to the mall, her short summer skirt lifting like a ribbed parasol. We ran across the tracks and across the far roadway onto the grass in front of the library, and looking at each other as if in confirmation, we turned and kept going past the benches of the bowling green and sat hard on the green itself, out of breath and smiling at each other until I reached over and kissed her on her open mouth.

"My God," she said, "I've got to go."

"Okay." But she didn't move, and when I kissed her again, she wound her arms around my waist, and I felt her clasped hands kneading my shirt. I held my breath. Then I reached up inside her blouse, under the ridge of the brassiere, to press my fingers against the base of her breasts. She drew away.

"My God! I've got to go, really."

"Okay. Okay. When can I see you?"

She rose and brushed her skirt from behind, with her legs braced apart. Her stance was provocative, unexpectedly. "You can't, John, I'm married. I mean, you know that."

"Tonight," I pleaded. "Come out on the south terrace tonight just before you clean up in the kitchen. Just before ten o'clock. I'll wait for you."

"I can't." She walked hurriedly back to the car tracks. "I can't," she called back to me.

"I'll wait for you," I shouted.

She got on the approaching car, which stopped to take her to the ferry.

That night I didn't look at Jean any of the times I went

in for my dinner orders. For almost three hours I was alternately made intense and distracted by the fear that I would not myself go to the terrace. I did not wonder, really, whether or not she would be there. Just before ten o'clock, when I picked up a tray on the second floor, I left it behind a stairwell and walked out to the terrace board-walk that circled the southwest corner of the hotel. I could barely hear the waves at low tide over the stray sounds coming from the game room on the other side of the patio, where bridge players talked and a phonograph played.

"John?"

"Yes."

"I can't stay long."

"What did you tell your husband?"

She didn't answer, and without seeing her face I knew I had touched her doubt.

"I'm sorry," I said.

"It's all right."

I stood looking at her uncertainly. She moved farther from the door and stood in space beneath the spotlight that shone outward toward the palms ten yards away. I saw her whole against the white slat framing of the build-ing, one leg bent so that her foot was flat against the wall, and both her palms also turned against it. She was ready. I leaned down and kissed her mouth and her closed eyes. She drew in her breath. Then we were quickly below the terrace, deep in the shadow of the building. We clung together, kissing, until she broke away and dropped to her knees and rocked back to lie on the thick grass. Her uni-form was gathered up to her waist, and I leaned into her while she clung to my neck, her knees held high, offering me her center. When it was over, both of us gasping, I stood up. She had said nothing. We turned away from each other to draw on our clothes. When I looked back, she was peering at me.

"You didn't say my name."

"Jean."

"Yes."

Chapter

6

After that it was easier and each day took shape before, anticipating its loss, I counted it. Nita said that I seemed to be easygoing. It was in the print shop, where I stopped in after the noon shift. What she said exactly was, "You know, you're not pressing."

"Pressing? I forget. Now, just what was your question, lady?" Nita laughed, shaking her head so that the points of her bobbed hair swirled in short arcs to her chin. That day I walked Nita back to the Greek's. She was off early and planned to do her wash before Spider came home. Now she asked if I wanted to see John Garfield in *Saturday's Children* at one of two movies on the boulevard. I said yes, for I knew already there was no chance of meeting Jean. As it turned out, I did not go because of poker.

At the Greek's you could play five-card draw or five-card stud, but you could not introduce exotic variations like Cincinnati that are thought to incite suspense in poker. If someone proposed to strip the deck of deuces and treys to liven the chances of drawing high cards, the Greek would say, "Listen, somebody like God made the deck fifty-two cards." We played jackpots strictly, jacks for openers. The Greek outlawed opening with a four flush or the four-card bobtail straight, and while he himself didn't favor the progression to queens and kings and aces in the event no one could open with jacks or two pairs or three of a kind, here the dealer could enforce his preference. The ante was repeated if no one could open.

The Greek didn't argue against playing hole-card stud, in which the first bet is made before the players look at the face-down card. Jackson was cynical about this dispensation. He said the Greek wasn't giving away much: being the house, he could play with less risk farther into the deck than others. The house was in the person of the Greek himself or Dolores, who would sit at the table without playing or else in the circle behind the players' chairs. The house share was one player's ante out of each pot. Jackson's conclusion was true but unimportant. The Greek was disciplined; everyone said he would not resist losing or winning just a little. I respected his puritanism. Poker is a game, like baseball, that ought to proceed meticulously until there occurs a sudden, telling action. Played right, it depends more on skill than on luck, but in the long run the winner is the skillful player who is not unlucky. I suppose that can be said also of metaphysicians and plumbers. As a prescription it is general, but then, I learned from reading William Hazlitt not to despise the obvious.

As for poker, I learned it from my father, who as a young man played obsessively in the coal fields of southern Illinois and Iowa and in Colorado. My mother told me with scorn that he once played for six days straight in a shack near the tipple of the Big Four coal mine outside Walsenburg, Colorado. By the time I was ten years old, he no longer played and explained poker as a pastime for bachelors, but I was impressed by his story of having played with a true professional, a certain Bulgar who, having sat one night through with my father, told him that he ought to learn to cheat or else quit, because he was not good enough to earn a living playing the game straight.

I got into the game about nine-thirty. By the time that Nita and Spider stopped by to go to the last show, I had already won three hands in a row. Spider watched a few minutes, half turned away from the table in his usual stiff stance, and when I won a pot piled with five-dollar red chips, he tugged Nita's sleeve and said quietly, "Let's go. He's got a run building." In the game there were five: a retired USN captain who lived on the island with a view of Cameron Island, where he once served as an aviator; two Loew's Theaters bosses from New York who had asked Shosh at the hotel to steer them to "the action" and told us that while they had meant girls, they were re-signed to cards; and the regular who ran a garage on the spit. The Greek looked liverish and sat back heavily in his chair at the table without taking a hand. We agreed to play draw poker with five-dollar antes and bets of two-five and two-five-fifteen, which means that before the discards and draw, the opening bet and raises have to be either two dollars or five dollars; but after the draw, the first bet and raises can be two or five or ten or the maximum, fifteen dollars. The New York men wanted higher stakes, and when they were overruled they retaliated by auto-matically raising the opening bet by five dollars should either one stay, the effect of which was to make an ordi-nary pot reach seventy-five dollars or more.

I sat down with eighty-five dollars—this out of the six hundred I had already saved or won playing cards during my seven weeks in California—and it was not long before I was ahead by seven hundred dollars, most of it won from the New York men. They were pretty good but impatient, forcing the game and making mistakes that may have followed on their being disdainful of the setting. One of them called the Greek's place a "deli," a word I'd never heard. Maybe they were just horny. Dolores left the table abruptly after a few hands and turned over the house to the Greek. I didn't notice her again until Nita and Spider returned at eleven-thirty.

Long before then, it was clear that the Loew's bosses were making poor moves to catch up. One of them would open with jacks when he was not the dealer, not a good idea even in a five-handed game, I think; both of them tended to raise the stakes pointlessly on low-card two pairs. I won three hundred thirty dollars by passing after I dealt myself two pairs—5♠, 5♥, and J♥, J♣, plus 9 ♣. As dealer I didn't hesitate to pass; on my left the captain also didn't open. One of the New York men opened with a five-dollar chip and both the garageman and the other New Yorker in turn raised five more, making it fifteen to me. I stayed. The captain dropped. After discards I dealt First New York two cards, the garageman one card, Second New York three cards, and myself one card, which I sliced into my hand face down without looking at it—a bush-league gesture that I dislike, though here I did it. First New York, whom I figured to hold three of a kind initially, bet fifteen, and the garageman raised fifteen, probably on a straight or flush, and Second New York raised fifteen—on what, it was hard to guess; maybe on having added an ace to a standing pair, or possibly drawing three to a full house, although the odds against that are stupefying. It was forty-five to me; I paid and raised fifteen. First New York raised fifteen, the garage-man paid and stayed, and Second New York raised fifteen and called: we all stayed to end it. I turned over my hand: 5♠, 5♥, 5♣, and J♥, J♣. First New York showed his openers, three nines, and the garageman groaned as he voluntarily turned over an open-end straight: 6♥, 7♦, 8♦, 9♦, 10♦. I had expected that, or else a diamond flush. Second New York didn't show his hand, but he squinted at me over the cigaret smoke that rose from his mouth. "Slicko," he said, "slicko. That room-service waiter. What did you call him, Shosher? You work with him, don't you?"

I stood up and as I reached behind me to clear my chair, the Greek said, "It ends this game," and motioned the pot toward me. "I don't much want to see your mouth full of fist," he said to the Loew's man, "not in my place."

"Come on, don't take it hard. Keep playing. It was just a joke."

"You're not funny enough," I said. "You ought to watch better movies." I swept the pot with the arc of my palm. That's when I saw Spider for the first time since his return. His eyes were brightly fixed on the pile of red and blue chips. I never before saw him so motionless. Once he sensed my looking at him, his face colored and he made an awkward about-face and walked quickly to the door. Dolores now looked at Nita in a tacit consolation. A few minutes later I found Spider leaning against the olive tree, his back to the store. Across the street the fronds of a palm tree flicked dryly against the lamppost, making the sounds of a steel brush on a snare drum.

"How was the movie?"

"Okay."

"Was Garfield, as usual, a tough guy?"

"I'm not sure. He wanted to get away."

"Like most people, he was, Spider; nobody stands still."

He looked up at me. "I don't rightly know. We use ta, home." He paused.

"You mean Nebraska, where your brothers are?"

"Naw. I mean Oklahoma, our farm." It struck me then that Okies can remain attached to the miserable places they'd left, places that were impermanent to them over several generations. For Spider and his kinfolks—chopping cotton at age eight or nine and on Saturday waiting for a piece of horehound candy under the red-rust tin porch of the general store in town, learning to walk sideways to the westerly wind that blew up dust as fine as flour—their tenant farm was their home, just as if it were owned and passed by legacy from father to son. For the first generation of emigrants, it was still home, for Spider and all those others who left, the straw-haired Scotch-Irish kids with flat faces who were right now on the road westward from Oklahoma and Kansas and eastern Colorado. Passing through Utah two months before, I had seen them in Model T's and Stars and Chevy trucks that cost three hundred and fifty dollars brand-new in 1931 and could be bought now secondhand for thirty or forty dollars. Running alongside Route 66, the Union Pacific heads northwest into Nevada. I was sitting on my hands, my feet dangling from the open door of an empty boxcar, when the Okies passed alongside. There were seven or eight to a car, their skin taffy brown from the color of the wind. I remember that one of them looked at me from startling eyes. With their felt hats and buttoned cotton coats they seemed to ride high, even though the cars were so heavily bundled with goods that the back ends sagged.

"Spider?"

"Yus?"

"I made more than a thousand bucks in there." He didn't reply. "I want to make you a small loan."

"I don't need no money."

"Well, maybe you don't need it, but I bet you could use it. You could have the Harley now."

"I ken wait."

"Sure. We all can. But why wait on a sure thing? You're going to buy it sooner or later. Let me lend you a hundred or so and you can pay me back over a couple of months. But you got to promise to quit playing the penny slots."

He grinned. "Well, hell. You mean it?" As if on a signal that the trading was done, we sat together on the curb and watched the light flicker.

"Did you ever drive a cycle? Back home, I mean," Spider asked.

"No. I'm a city kid. I didn't drive a car until I was fourteen; that's when I learned to swim, too, which has a connection."

"There's nuthin ain't like it, Big John. See, it's not like drivin' a car or truck. You feel the piston right up thu your feet. It's like you had long arms and legs. One time I rid one out of Altus, back in Oklahoma. I wus goin' a ninety mile an hour and could see near twenty mile ahead. I left so much dust I wus all alone."

"Did you own it?"

"Naw. It was an Indian motorcycle my brother had once until he sol' it."

The next day I gave Spider one hundred and fifteen dollars, to which he added sixty-five more to buy a new Harley-Davidson from a store on Fourth Avenue in San Diego, a monster machine with a big black saddle and red-and-blue-and-white enameled tank and mudguards. The chrome felt thick and oily smooth on the handlebars

67

and spokes and pedals and on the exhaust pipes that thrust backward like long scoops. Right off, Spider began a routine. Overnight he kept the Harley in the alley back of the Greek's and every morning and evening he would signal his departure by revving up with a sound that impacts and exhales, like a jackhammer powered by a gas generator. On Sundays Spider would lay a piece of tarp that Jackson had lifted from naval stores at Cameron Island; on it he carefully placed the dismantled parts of the Harley, cleaning and oiling and brushing and tightening one by one to a succession of assenting sounds: "Yup," "Hum-yup," "Uh-huh," "Hell yus," "Okay."

Jackson sometimes offered to help, his qualification being not only that he stole the tarp but also that he was a former cycle rider. Spider politely refused. "You would think he was operating on his mother's brain," Jackson complained to me as we stood watching Spider. "One slip of the wrench and the old girl is gone." Only once, during an afternoon when he was off work, did Spider try to furbish the Harley in front of the store. The Greek banned him after listening to the first ten minutes of the exquisitely excruciating tuning of the engine, the whispers forced by a turn of the handle to a roar, the percussion deepening from idle taps to a hammering, each sound confiding to Spider subtle symptoms of the Harley's readiness.

Spider tried to work in front because Nita wouldn't stay in the alley with him. She had no interest in what made the motorcycle run and was impatient that its starting required intricate effort. She looked amused while Spider's hands and feet ran through a scale of feeding gas, setting and resetting the ignition and choke, kicking the starter five or six times. But once Spider and the Harley were ready, Nita jumped on quickly, surely. Every day she could be seen clutching Spider high on the chest, her bare legs straddling the machine so hard that her thighs were pressed flat, their tendons showing like small ropes. As Spider eased the Harley out of the driveway next to the store, Nita would wave to anyone looking down from the rooms or out the store windows. Then they would bank steeply and burst into the street, Nita holding her head to one side, her hair strung out like short wings, her mouth open, thrilled.

Others rode with Spider at times. He never lent the Harley, but he would give anyone who asked a ride up to the streetcar on the boulevard; on occasion he took people across the ferry as far as the Naval Hospital in Balboa Park, or to the new County Building on Harbor Drive. It seems odd now that I never rode with Spider, but then, I spent a lot of time trying to see Jean. It soon occurred to me that more hours were in fact spent in our making and revising plans to meet than in being together. When I complained, she said regretfully but without apology that she had to manage both her job and her husband. Within days of our having made love below the hotel terrace, we agreed that I could safely see her in only two places: on the beach about a half mile from where she and George lived with his parents, and in San Diego when she had a day off. Meeting for a few minutes at places about the hotel was not impossible but dangerous. Jean warned that George knew everyone on the hotel staff except the Filipinos; and of course his mother patrolled the upper floors as a housekeeper and his father was about, helping Harry. We both feared discovery, but for Jean there was something more. I'm sure she recognized that the risk and brevity of our meeting in secret places would turn into a hungry sexual encounter, making us thieves on the grab and run, as we had been that first time on the grass. We never spoke of that night. Jean was not one to use her memories. Thinking of this, I was proud but also jealous that Jean, unlike me, would not introduce a question of reputation into our intrigue.

Nonetheless, as there was no other way, we had to speak at work to set dates. I could hardly telephone the Fancher house, and Jean had no girl friend at work. Eventually I chose Leonid as a go-between because from his vantage at the bake ovens he could see both Jean and me on those days, rarer now, when I went into the kitchen between shifts. Maybe he chose himself. Leonid had inferred enough to confront me: "You are crazy for that yellow girl, Johnny," he kept saying, using the word "yellow" for blond the way some Slavs do. I told Jean I was willing to confide in him if she agreed, yet I hesitated because I am meticulous in a sense of how things go wrong. I routinely invoke scenes of letters undelivered, schedules not posted, ambulances proceeding to wrong addresses while people lie dying. What if Leonid started to give Jean a message in his broken English and, sensing that she did not comprehend, started to shout, as one does at foreigners and children? Or, failing to find her, what if he wrote a message on a slip of paper that became attached to the wet underside of a tray to be discovered by a room-service waiter, who would give it to her butcher husband—just for fun.

We lay on the beach and made love and shared a certain silence. We walked the streets of San Diego and rode the streetcar uphill to the zoo. One day we stood on the sand below the arched span of the Crystal Pier at Pacific Beach and listened to the tinny music coming from the little blue cottages lined in a row on the pier like houses drawn with crayons on gray school paper. Away from her, I grew anxious that she might become deprived. She deserved—how keenly I felt it!—an unexpected joy. It was not on my part, I think, in any way condescension or other grandness. I recognized that the pleasure she gave to me was unmixed, for when I left her for the day, while I went about unrelated things, she had always to return to the Fanchers. I persisted in having difficulty comprehending her apart from the Fanchers; and I felt oppressed by her being married, probably because there was no way I could avoid knowing that sexually she was more experienced than I. Though I had read George Gissing and Somerset Maugham, it was hard to conclude that my experience, not Jean's, was at issue whenever I felt the awkwardness of our relationship.

The fact is that I hardly knew anything about married women—the mothers of your acquaintances do not count in this respect. What little I knew came from two occasions, one ridiculous and the other so elemental that from it I learned nothing at all. As a twelve-year-old student in junior high school, when I was five and one-half feet tall and overweight, I fell in love with my homeroom teacher, Miss Desmond, who was tall and lithe and whose dark-brown marcelled hair fit her like a bathing cap. She looked like those women who stood in front of LaSalle V-8's in magazine ads. Had I been asked her age, I would have said more than thirty, but she was in fact twenty-four. Eight years later, when I was a senior at the university, I took the former Miss Desmond, now Mrs. Tillotson, who was separated from her husband, to a college dance and kissed her passionately on the back seat of a four-door Ford convertible I borrowed from a fraternity brother.

I had met her the weekend before at a sorority house where I worked as a waiter and was surprised that I recognized her immediately: she was spectacular, still slim, her head inclined expectantly, like Nefertiti. At first she declined my invitation because it was a bother for her to take the train from our home city. Her husband, she said, had selfishly kept their car. But I pressed and she agreed, and the whole week was left to me to wonder nervously if I could take advantage of her experience. But it was my prejudice, not hers, that started us off badly. Picking her up at the station, stopping for drinks at the house of a bachelor professor, and at the dance, I found myself steadily dismayed that my Miss Desmond was boring and had not the least intellectual interest in the typicalities of society. After the dance she consented to necking in the car but argued against going "all the way," because it would be "unnatural" for a woman who had known me as a child. I told her the argument was illogical because some girls my own age knew me as a child. Nothing came of it. I accept that it could have been worse had she heard of Freud.

Otherwise, not much, not much at all. One winter my father and I spent the night in the house of a Serbian lodge member, a coal miner who came from Banat in the Old Country. He was older than my father, maybe sixty at the time, but his wife was at least twenty-five years younger. She was a dark and musky woman. Somehow I got the impression that she was turbulent, even though she rarely spoke or looked directly at anyone—not at me at least. After an evening of listening to my father's friends complain of the reactionary bent of Prince Paul, the Regent of Yugoslavia, I'd gone to bed upstairs in a spare room among the fifteen or so rooms that my father's friend and his wife kept as a boardinghouse for miners. Before dawn I heard the rustlings of a coal-camp rooming house as it came awake to the sounds of water, huge kettles being filled and set on the coal stoves in the kitchen below, the pump working up and down in the backyard, the muffled slosh of slop jars in the rooms, and a sound like glass breaking as a stream of piss fell to the icy ground from the window just above mine.

By six-fifteen the house was silent, all the men gone to the tipple. I heard my father's Model A start up as he went alone to visit a nearby town where an old lodge member was laid up by a broken leg. He had quietly left our room, having mercy on my sleep, probably putting on his high-top shoes and leather leggings down in the kitchen. I had slipped back into dreaming when I felt her next to me in the rough sheets. She was naked. Her skin was at first taut from the cold of the room's air, but it loosened and felt oily by the time her hands had worked me up. Before I could search for her nipples with my mouth she was astride me, heaving and swaying, her hair and her breasts slapping my face as I strained upward. Her rough heels dug into my thighs, releasing me only slightly to match her rhythm. She was off me and gone through the door before I could slow my breath, which was visible in the gray air of the morning. Not a word had passed. I never saw her again.

If the truth were told, and it was not, I was surprised that it did not alter our love-making that Jean had been to bed hundreds of times—I figured it out painfully by multiplying the seventy-six weeks they had been married against the number of times a week I guessed George Fancher would make demands. Yet she seemed as nearly virginal as I, and I began to regard her experience as

73

having been forced upon her and therefore incalculable and not indelible. It came about, reluctant as she was to talk about her husband and obligingly disinterested as she seemed when I talked about my own simple past, that I was less and less concerned that she lay with another man.

I entered into qualified speculations on what might happen to us, but not even indecisiveness could suppress my present delight. Just what I conveyed to Jean I cannot be sure, for she never asked for confessions of intimacy. Afterward, I think I felt most seriously that she was owed gladness. I know what impelled my wish. I was recognizing, without at the time being able to formulate it, that Jean was the most reliably virtuous person of my age I had known. She credited my ambitions as my own, but if she had long-standing hopes beyond our being together, she did not let them fall upon the moment.

Chapter

7

If you came back late at night from Tijuana, the United States border guards did not volunteer touring instructions, for they assumed you were citybound, headed straight north up the mainland to San Diego or Los Angeles. Chula Vista was a possibility, I suppose, but it was more of a Jack Benny joke than a place to visit. Even going to San Diego an uneven choice presented itself, for you could turn left on the turtleback cement road and reach the Pacific Ocean at Imperial Beach. From there you could go north along the spit of land that ran to the island, blocking the ruffled white edge of the ocean from the calm black of San Diego Bay. The highway ended at the circle in front of the hotel, and having come this far, you had to follow the boulevard to the ferry. The spit, you see, was a small peninsula, maybe legitimately the tip of Baja California.

I know this salty spine of land well, not just from swimming on South Beach with Elizabeth and Shosh and the others. It is the place Jean lived with the Fanchers and where we met twice a week through Jean's skillful management. She left the house most mornings at six-thirty with her father-in-law; she got off work at three but waited for him until five. George drove his mother up to the hotel at ten-thirty and both of them stayed until eight. Jean used the gaps in these schedules for our meetings. At three I'd borrow Harry's car and we'd go to Silver Strand Beach, about two thousand yards from her house. She explained her ability to get home early by inventing a new-found girl friend with a car who worked on the island and lived at Imperial Beach. On Jean's late shift, when she had more than two hours off during the afternoon, we could together leave the island.

Jean typically did not plead its complication, but I wondered at the logistics of all this. I was relieved that things worked out, quite contrary to tendency, but I expect that I was also amazed that being with a girl could be technically simple; since puberty my imagination had been frustrated by considering the obstacles of meeting a girl secretly and then manfully getting past brassieres, slips, garter belts, stockings, panties—contrived variously by buttons and bands and snaps and slides. By the time I was in college I espoused the mechanistic theory of unequal return, that a little passion is like small crime. When I asked Jean how she expected George to accept the sudden presence of a girl friend with a car, she said, "I never told George or his folks a lie before; they've got no reason not to trust me." She did not say that the Fanchers were not notably watchful. George was jealous, as all in the kitchen knew, but he was so testily single-minded that his temper was not broadened by observation. His mother complained about her health persistently and was in consequence uninterested in others. As for Elmore, I told Harry once, "He's like a Stillson wrench. He has to reset himself to get ahold of anything."

Jean and I met on Silver Strand out of sight of the Fancher house, which sat back from the highway on the bay side among four or five other frame houses all covered by red asbestos sheets scored to look like brickwork. The beach was always deserted in the afternoon. Nobody fished from the shore or dug clams. Isolated, we lay between blankets on the fine sand, our heads against the hillocks that were stuck with strands of beach grass like chin whiskers. Everything was steady here. Even the color of the seascape did not change except when the wind blew hard or fog drifted. At the land's edge lay a bed of orange pebbles, sorted and worn, and next to it the plaster-gray walk where the breakers crossed. The sea was an uneven purple and weed-brown for about a mile out, until it turned dependably blue.

"What do you see out there, Jean?"

"Nothing, really. China, maybe."

"I seem never to think about China."

"My father was in China as a Navy chief. When I was little I heard him talk about the China Station and I thought it was a big open building, like Union Station in L.A., full of Chinamen."

"Have you ever been on a boat?"

"I was once. A Navy launch. My father took me to San Clemente Island. He had a friend who had duty at a place called Seal Harbor. Only a little Navy place with rocks and mossy hills. It was lonely."

"No," I said, "it was empty. You were lonely."

"You're using words against me again, Johnny. It's the same. Still and all, I suppose it is different in New York and Philadelphia, all those millions of people in old cities. Out here it seems vacant at times."

I looked out at the islands fifteen miles off the coast—

are they part of Mexico or California? They are like a black stone giant lying in shallow water with only his waist submerged. It struck me then that there is a subjective identity to places apart from the presence of people. I'd never been to the East or to England, but I was sure that a place with hardwood trees and full rivers and fine grass that isn't each year reseeded can never seem as lonely to the viewer as the flat, dry plains or the foothills in the West. Was it true inside cities, too? There was something abandoned about the kind of street where Jean grew up in Compton, where the small stucco semibungalows were alike but kept their distance and held an unremarkable silence. I saw streets like that after I left the island and went to L.A.—from Lynwood and Watts and Gardena through downtown. Would e. e. cummings or H. L. Mencken recognize those streets? No.

"How come you lived in Compton?"

"My mother has her sister there. Because my father was away a lot, she wanted to be close. When we moved to San Diego—my dad was stationed in boot camp then—she kept going back to Compton on visits and after I graduated from high school she left for good."

"Was it for good?"

Jean smiled tightly. "I suppose it was. I don't miss her much. I'm sorry for that. She always said I could be in the movies because she thinks I look like Lana Turner."

"You do. You just haven't found the right drugstore."

"I ended up at the naval air station on Cameron Island and married George." She said it without a suggested regret, but how could she? It was only about a year ago, but I imagined her, as if from distant time, standing and walking purposefully in the disbursing office on Cameron, keeping neat ledgers on the pay and allowances of sailors and meeting George only accidentally because he worked as a butcher in the commissary. She had been nineteen, with a body so fresh and so full that she could not dress demurely if she tried. Earlier she had told me that all through high school she was rubbed and poked and grabbed in petting encounters but never finally reached until George took her.

"For God's sake," I said in anger of its recollection. "You didn't have to get married because of that."

"No, but I was pregnant. After I married George and we moved in with his folks, I had a miscarriage."

"You didn't love him."

"No. But it doesn't change things."

"How can you say that?"

"I love you, Johnny. Does it make any difference?" I couldn't see her eyes because her cheek was against my chest. "It's not your fault that I'm married. It's not even George's fault."

"But you won't stay with him, will you?"

She didn't answer, and our resolution was to make love, sharing our talents. She was not patient and sometimes could hardly bear my kissing her mouth for long, but she taught me to use her whole body, which at first I avoided out of fear, whether original to me or vestigial I cannot know. Her body was astonishing, more secret than I thought possible, and more variable: her breasts and buttocks and belly swelled when the blood pounded in her. When her skin was suffused, her long neck and the hollows at her waist were firmly exquisite. I never tired of tracing her figure with my hands. On the days we walked in downtown San Diego or went to Ocean Beach, I would rest my forearm on her shoulder and gently hold the nape of her neck between my thumb and forefinger; it made me feel that I could at the same time hold her and guide her.

At first Jean wouldn't let me kiss her on the streetcar or the ferry when we crossed the bay, mindful that our fellow hotel workers might be aboard, but she relented because I argued that our being together could itself cause suspicion. When there was little time, we would do no more than ride the ferry, standing at the side rail to look at the gray shapes of destroyers and minelayers and, looming, the *Lexington*. Across the bay we could see white and pink buildings stuck in the greenery that rose street by street from Golden Hill up to Balboa Park. Other days, when there was more time, we walked down C Street to find a movie to watch intermittently, out of an obligation not to waste the price of admission, while I kissed her eyes and mouth. We sat on the benches in the small city park off Broadway. It was not neat like the library and bowling green on the island, but before twilight it was made lively by sailors on liberty, who got off the streetcar that runs north from the base and met here in groups to argue and dissemble over their strategies for the night. If it rained hard, Jean and I ran to the little belvedere at the center of the park. The white wood columns were surrounded by a stone fountain that required our wading to reach the painted floor under the cupola.

"They've got no place to go," I commented on the sailors. "It's like recess, isn't it? I remember junior high school. Mine was a big new one. When the weather was not good, they would herd us out of the cafeteria onto an asphalt roof with a rail around it, like a prison yard in the movies."

"Did you like school?"

"I don't remember a day that I didn't like it. If I ever

write my memoirs, I probably won't admit that. All writers say they had a miserable time at school."

"I didn't know that. Maybe good times aren't interesting."

"Well, if ever I write, I'll tell my mother's story. She grew up hard."

"Not your father?"

"He had a tough time," I said, "but he feels at home with his people. He misses the coal mines because of that."

"Do you know the coal mines?"

"Not to live there, though I was born in a company town. I've gone with my father to the camps to see his lodge members. One time we went to Gebo, in Wyoming. We went to the house of a Serb miner for supper. The younger women stood around and served and didn't themselves eat until we were finished. I was about thirteen. I remember standing at the beginning, waiting for the old women to be seated, until my father said to me in a stern whisper, 'Sit down! These are Montenegrins and they are honoring your manhood.' "

"It's the nicest story I ever heard." Jean liked accounts of my childhood and would cue my reminiscing, but I noticed she didn't care to hear about my college days, because they must have seemed less characteristic. It was bound to be, perhaps, because college makes a difference between those who go and those who can't. How does it happen? Do college people carry to old age a protracted recollection of dormitory rooms, of fraternity dances, of spring weekdays sitting on the grass and afternoon dates? Does it separate them tacitly from people who have never taken a vacation, these favored ones who dozens of times have packed matched suitcases, gone back and forth,

changing the venue of their lives? Talking to Jean I realized with disquiet, for the first time, I think, that formal
learning is not mainly at issue: it is not full-time college
but full-time campus.

Without reference to Jean, I said something of this to
Harry and Leon about three weeks after I began seeing
her regularly. I still stopped at Harry's office behind the
latticework before going to the children's dining room.
Sergio continued to ask me to fill in and I consented,
though I was less in need of money than before and also
less obliged, for Arthur had long since gone home to Hollywood. Good tips were still to be had there. I waited on
Robert Young's children for a couple of weeks and was
given forty dollars by his wife, who was about thirty years
old and caused Shosh to say, when he saw her in her tennis
shorts, "She looks pretty great for an older woman." On
the way to Harry's office I ran into Leon once or twice and
asked him to join us even though he and Harry had nothing to say to each other. Harry didn't mind too much, I
think, and Leon was delighted to talk about American
institutions; he complained that no one in the hotel was
"serious."

"College," I told Harry, "is based on the principle of
leisure."

"Now just what in hell does that mean?"

"I'm talking about class structure."

"That I agree," said Leon.

"For Christ sake," Harry said to both of us.

"Listen, Harry: how is it that it took me four years to do
college studies that on a nine-to-five job could have been
done easily in a year?"

"I give up. Why?"

"Because all the campus stuff is luxury. Leisure time

with steady meals is what makes a middle and upper class."

"That's highly true," Leon added with pleasure, his eyes narrowing at the thought. "Rich people. They don't work."

"They don't work *all* the time," Harry said to me, not Leon. "Some of the time they stay in hotels like this one." He lit a cigaret end to end, scattering sparks when he pinched off the old butt.

"That's right," I said.

"So what's the point?"

"The point, Harry, is that because class distinction is one result of it, education is not considered a form of work."

"I can't understand that." Harry kicked the tripod of his swivel chair to swing himself around directly facing me. "Tell me, kid, do you give a crap about that class stuff?"

I laughed, to Leon's surprise. "No, Harry, I don't. When I was in college my notion of a bad time was listening to an agitated girl denouncing the class society. I once went with a girl who said she had to love me less than the Communist party. She wouldn't give her life for me."

"You didn't ask enough. That's your trouble."

Harry knew that did not apply to him, for I was borrowing his car regularly. For a time he'd just look at me blankly, making the silence heavy, as he handed me the keys. After a while he was saying, "Keep the seats inside the car, damn it!" Or, "If she kicks out the windshield, John, I'll have your ass." By the time I admitted I was seeing Jean—I decided to confide in Harry rather than lose access to his car—my confidence was not really a trust, for my routine was established and Harry had deduced it. Soon, when we had a smoke together in the morning, Harry was talking to me about the Fanchers as if they were disreputable relatives of mine. He liked my listening. I liked it, too.

"The old man," Harry said of Elmore, "has been working the hotel for about twenty years. He was a stoker when we had coal furnaces here. Them days a coal barge would come across the bay from the Twenty-eighth Street Pier and Elmore and another guy, who's dead now, would unload the coal onto a belt that I rigged to an old White twenty-horse engine. When we bought oil burners about five years ago, old Elmore came to work direct for me. He ain't bright, but he's not noisy either.

"But George, he should have been a marine at Camp Pendleton. He's a born MP. He'd be happy walking downtown Dago in white leggins, with a stick and a gun on white cords. You've seen those peckerwoods, lookin' in bars for sailors to bust their heads. I remember when I was in Navy Fuel Supply on Point Loma, a Marine MP come up on me while I was waiting for the interurban and tapped me across the small of my back with his stick. I ducked my head and grabbed his stick and stuck it right in his balls. The dumb bastard never got a look at me because by then his own head was down. I never was up on captain's mast, that time or no other.

"But about Elmore and George and their rumrunnin'. Back about nineteen twenty-five it was, there was a lot of booze run over the border. In the movies you see guys like George Bancroft and Chester Morris haulin' the stuff in boats from the ocean, which may be okay in New York or New Jersey or wherever, but it wasn't like that here. That's not to say that booze wasn't being run on the bay, but the bay stops three miles short of the border, so you can't load up in Tijuana, say, and chug right up to Dago.

What happened was this. The Mex runners would carry the white whiskey on dirt roads out of Agua Caliente and come up into the U.S. through the canyons on the far side of Otay. Otay is a crappy little place, a couple of streets without a stop sign. They stashed the white stuff there, coloring it with burnt sugar and aging it a couple of days before they put on those eight-year labels. Then they put the booze on inboards and on a dark night, especially with fog drifting in, they'd run it up. The Coast Guard had boats out of Shelter Island and once in a while they'd catch them, or, more likely, run into them. It can get so dark on the bay you can't find a way in—even if it has hair around it.

"It was about thirty-two, I guess, not ten years ago, when the Fanchers got to thinking they were left out. George was about twenty-five then. He'd been in Kansas City, married, I think, and come back to work on Cameron. By then booze was being run by cars, so they bought a strong car, a Dodge Eight coupe with eighty-five horse and a double-drop frame. It cost them twelve hundred bucks, a hell of a lot in the Depression. George got the idea to box out a space behind the seat where they could stash five-gallon tins of booze. They were all set. Their idea, see, was to drive the booze up to the hotel and sell it to the guests through the room-service waiters, which is like getting Aimee Semple McPherson to give the word to five thousand revenue agents.

"Elmore was getting nervous. Here they were with a fast car and no place to go. They asked me if I knew any Mex bootleggers. Dumb. Finally, somebody told them about a guy in Otay who knew somebody who knew somebody else and they made a connection. George went out and bought a black-and-white-checked suit with a vest, like he was George Raft. As it turned out, they would drive down to Caliente, fill the back of the Dodge with tins of white gin, and drive back over the border sloshing all the way. Christ! They must have sounded like a drunk in a tub. After a while the Mexes began to hustle them. No more booze, they said, unless George and Elmore would every now and then carry a Mex in that box in the coupe. Just a little case of smuggling aliens.

"One night in Caliente they were supposed to pick up a guy on a corner. They saw this old guy in a white suit with long hair. He was drunk stiff, barely standing, but he spoke to them in Spanish when they got to him, and since they figured that only Spics speak Spanish, they wrestled this old guy into the back and knocked him out so he'd keep quiet. By the time they crossed the border, they found out from his wallet that they'd kidnapped the American consul at Caliente. Now they were scared, so they carried him to the hotel and stashed him in an empty room that Elmore's wife unlocked for them. The head housekeeper found him in the hall the next morning in his white suit but no shoes, saying over and over, 'I have been recalled! What a disgrace!'

"The story must have got back to the Mexes in Caliente. What happened was that Elmore and George went back to pick up booze, and when they got to Tijuana, Elmore remembers suddenly that his wife made him promise to bring back fireworks—the Mexes are both good and cheap with fireworks. They stopped at the border with the ledge under the back window of the coupe packed with rockets and cherry bombs and all that crap. A guard leaned in and got interested in the fireworks. By this time George was worried, and he lit a cigar. I forgot to say that he'd started chewing cigars about the time he got the checked suit.

One way or another, George managed to light a sparkler, which fell into the crack to the back. There was an explosion so big it blew itself out. Elmore broke his arm and wasn't worth a damn to me for a month. George only lost his checked suit—and the Dodge, of course. The guard was put in the hospital, but nobody arrested the Fanchers because, you see, it wasn't booze but pure gasoline that they were carrying in those tins. The Mexes had put George and Elmore out of business permanent.

"I wouldn't expect much good to come of your screwing around, kid. Those Fanchers are plain unlucky."

Chapter

8

It was the last half of August and everybody I knew was still in place. The summer season was closing within weeks but the hotel was full and staging more "events" than usual, notably a summer cotillion attended by affluent families from as far away as Long Beach and a tennis tournament that brought writers and actors and actresses from Hollywood. My friend the barman said that they coupled and recoupled like free freight cars all weekend long. By this time I had given up my children's dining room second job because I needed more time with Jean, and I found I could profitably work the pool and tennis courts. In room service I kept my usual numbers and angled for lucrative new ones like the songwriters Johnny Mercer and Jimmy Van Heusen, who occupied a suite for two weeks while writing songs for a movie. They were perhaps the only people I saw at the hotel that summer who came solely to work. Over lunch and during the afternoon they banged on an upright piano installed in the sitting room and bantered over the lyrics while phrasing the music. Coming in and out with meals and drinks, I heard bits of their arguments and was particularly surprised that they were serious about the motivations of the characters in a movie musical. Van Heusen said to me, "Do you think that a jilted girl would sing a song wishing that she was older?" I asked, "How much older is the other woman?" "Bingo, Jimmy," Mercer called out triumphantly. They went back to Hollywood the next day. When they left, Van Heusen told me the big tip was for my criticism, not for the cold kippers.

This was the same week that I came back from Silver Strand about six—Jean told the Fanchers she'd visited her friend at Imperial Beach—and was late reporting to the tennis courts. Sergio threatened me with dismissal, not for the first time. He told the second chef that I was "not professional" and could never make a captain, which he took to be a legitimate ambition of mine. He had not noted, or else ignored, that college graduates will work in an office as an assistant manager at less pay rather than remain as waiters. Perhaps Sergio could not credit that some of us actually had university standing. We were not, after all, lawyers or professors—not the sort of people called "Dottore"—obviously not wellborn, for nobody had ever heard of us and we were not even known to each other. When Sergio threatened me I told him not to be "operatic," and since he could hardly find another waiter at the end of the summer, he did not persist. "You are all alike," he cried angrily, making my misdemeanor a generic failure, retreating from a broad front rather than concede a hand-to-hand encounter.

That afternoon I stayed late at the courts. The tournament matches had ended and no more than ten people were at nearby tables. Each time I brought drinks from the bar, it was to a diminished group. When dusk fell there was no one left at the tables to watch Pancho Segura in the center court lazily trading shots with a powerful boy of sixteen. Segura lobbed the ground strokes, and the exchange would continue until the boy missed an overhand out of his eagerness to smash a ball into irretrievability. There was but one spectator. I recognized him as Nigel Bruce, the Dr. Watson of a series of very good B movies. He leaned out the third-story window of the hotel overlooking the courts, giving encouragement to the boy with an occasional "Bravo" or "I say." I remember them exactly: Segura in mock disgust sailing his racket high into the violet air and, overhead, Bruce framed in a niche like a Roman.

It was so late that I went straight on duty for the dinner hour, and had made two trips when I came down the stairs carrying an empty heater. I saw Nita standing in the corridor near the checker's kiosk. She was in the way of traffic, her legs spread, her hands clasped at her sides. She looked that way when we played volleyball on the sand. As I drew near I could see that her lips were pressed against trembling.

"Nita?"

"It's Spider."

"Where is he?"

"In Indio."

"Indio? What's he doing there?"

"He went out to see his brother in Las Vegas, he said."

"Well, he's coming back."

"That's not it, Johnny. He's hurt."

"How do you know? Maybe it's a mistake."

"A hospital in Indio called the Greek's." I waited and looked down at Nita, still holding the heater and having it banged against my leg as waiters brushed by closely. "He had a wreck on his motorcycle."

"Jesus!"

"Will you go with me, Johnny? I mean to Indio?"

"Sure. We'll go now. Have you got any money on you?"

"I forgot. I ran all the way from the Greek's."

"It's okay. I'll get some." I left her there to borrow twenty dollars from Leonid and to talk the assistant cashier into giving me twenty dollars advance against my paycheck due the following day. When I got back, Nita was still in the corridor, Sergio standing next to her but obviously disdaining her.

He said to me, "Why the hell? You must be working."

"Pay attention, Sergio. If you get in my way, I may paste you in the mouth."

He stood at the head of the outside stairs, above the employment office, as Nita and I ran across the lawn to the boulevard streetcar stop. As I looked back, he seemed to me almost pensive.

Nita and I caught a bus at the station that was headed for San Bernardino and Barstow on Route 395. We didn't calculate much in choosing this bus; there is a better connection in Los Angeles for Indio, but either way we could not reach the hospital that night. There had been no question of my asking Harry for his car. It was a long, hard trip and I'd be asking a loan, not a favor. Somehow I knew that Harry would not collaborate in Nita's favor. He was strict when he talked of his own daughters. We boarded at ten o'clock and rode silently in the moonlight as the bus climbed the valley north to the little orderly town of Escondido. Nita was asleep on my shoulder as we passed out of the avocado groves rising to the dry scrub hills, the chaparral.

The bus reached Riverside at three in the morning, dropping us off at the station to wait for our connection, an eight-o'clock bus going east on Highway 60 to Indio. There was nothing to do but sit awake or sit sleeping, for the benches were cruelly divided by bolted metal arms that prevented the sober and the drunk alike from sleeping stretched out. The coffee shop was long ago closed, and Nita resisted my suggestion that we look for an all-night diner, as if leaving the station was deviant to our mission. We sat staring at the empty ticket counter, the round classroom clock, the Wrigley's posters. When the sun came up I persuaded Nita to walk outside. Across from the station, beyond Market Street and a grass mall, we found one of those grandiose buildings usually dated 1928 or 1929 that you grasp immediately to be too ambitious for their settings. This one, called Mission Inn, was built of gray concrete with spired or capped towers unevenly spaced; corridors burrowed into it from all sides, and galleries hung where there were no windows. It was a great sand castle abandoned in the early-morning light. I was delighted by it and left Nita standing on the sidewalk as I bounded up the main staircase. Stuck on the staircase walls were enameled chivalric shields of no recognizable orders—one of them engraved "1930"—and crossed swords made of pewter. Nearby were pulpitlike boxes supported on ornate protruding bosses. I went down to tell Nita that the Mission Inn was a most marvelously misnamed place. It was an office building, hotel, apartment house, and whatever else it could become by lien.

"What are you playing?" she asked sharply. "Hide-and-seek?" We didn't talk again when we boarded the bus for Indio or stopped at Beaumont for breakfast with the other passengers. It was hot, over one hundred degrees at nine in the morning. Inside the small café the flies scouted the dirty glass covers of the cake stands. I ate eggs and potatoes smelling of white frying fat while Nita stared and smoked. As we got back on the bus, I felt displaced. I did not belong in Beaumont, California, with thirty-three dollars in my pocket and a dark silent girl at my side whose aching fear, it could be seen in her eyes, would subside only when she was made certain of fact. She and I were detached, adjoining but separated, like the bus and the Southern Pacific train trundling on the tracks parallel to the highway.

As it entered the desert the bus settled to the road from pressure of heat. The view danced ahead. The desert was not colorless from a distance, or bare: on the hills were yellow plants called century and paloverde trees and the white flame of yucca, which must have been named by some lost traveler "Our Lord's Candle." I picked these out from the scrub and the mesquite quite deliberately, trying to arm myself against strangeness. Arriving at the station in Indio did not help. The air was stale. The heat seemed particulate, with motes suspended in a thin white vapor. On the instructions of an old man who sat, incredibly, in the open light outside the tiny bus station, Nita and I found the hospital a block south of Route 60. It was a small one-story building that looked more a veterinary's place than a real hospital, although it did have Venetian blinds.

"The name is Corey," I told the woman at the small telephone board inside the entrance. I hadn't known Spider's surname until just before we went in.

"Wait jes a minute," she said. A man came out wearing a white shirt with short sleeves and with two pens clipped to its pocket.

"Are you relatives?"

"Yes," Nita said quickly.

"I'm sorry," he said.

Nita stared at him, the hollow in her throat deepening. "Did he wake up?" she asked finally.

"No. He was brought in by the highway police unconscious. I didn't try to operate. His neck was broken: the third vertebra was smashed. He could not have felt anything."

"Where is he now?" I asked after Nita had turned away and as the doctor looked at his watch.

"He's at the undertaker's on the main street, Halsted's. But you'll have to go over to the highway police station, too. They've got Corey's things and the motorcycle, what's left of it."

There was something left. Nita insisted she go alone to the undertaker's so that I could stop at the state police station. A sergeant with orange patches on his shoulders took me out back where the Harley was chained against a standpipe, strangely undamaged except for a skewed front wheel and toed-in front forks. I asked him, explaining that there was no way to get a relative of Spider's to Indio, if I could sign for his things: a wallet, a brass ring, and two chrome pants clips. He agreed when I gave him Harry's address and offered to pay for a call to the island to vouch for my identity. But he said he'd have to ask the lieutenant, who was away, about the Harley. When I got back to the undertaker's, a white house with yellow awnings over a deep porch, Nita met me at the front door and drew me aside.

"What do I do, Johnny? Do we wait to send a telegram to Spider's folks? I don't know where the brother is in Las Vegas. How long can we wait?"

"What did the undertaker say?"

"He says in two days he'll have to turn Spider over to the county to bury him."

"How much does he want?"

"I forgot to ask."

"We'll do this, Nita: we'll pay him something down for the funeral. Then we can wait for his folks to come."

"I don't have any money."

"Well, don't worry about it. If I have to, I'll call Harry to wire money, but I've got an idea that the police will give us the Harley and we can sell it for enough to hold the undertaker."

That's the way it worked out. The lieutenant listened to the story, which Nita's somber presence seemed to sanctify, and he agreed to release the motorcycle. The larger of two garages in town paid seventy dollars for the cycle, out of which I paid sixty-five to the undertaker, spent a dollar to wire Nebraska, and two more for a tourist cabin on the far side of Indio. I told Nita I would rent two cabins but she refused on the grounds of economy: I would have to lend her money so she could remain in town waiting on Spider's folks after I went back the next morning. Our cabin was a box made of gray unpainted pine boards nailed to two-by-four studs with no inside finishing wall. It held an iron bed, an old chiffonier, a kitchen chair. It was too hot to sit inside. My God, it was hot! I could hardly accept the signals of my senses. I told myself that Indio is at sea level on the edge of a bowl of sand and scrub, the center of which is the Salton Sea. But placing the heat did nothing to lessen its effects. Nita and I sat in the filling-station office in front of the cabins, where there was a slow-turning overhead fan and an automatic coin icebox that held barely cooled bottles of pop.

95

After sundown we went back to stand by Spider at the undertaker's—I'd paid another five bucks so that he could be dressed in a shirt and trousers—but unaccountably it was closed and no one answered even at the back door. We returned to the cabin, which was a little less stifling after sundown but still not really tolerable. I took off my shirt and shoes and socks; the shoes were stained through with sweat. I sat on the stoop with the screen door open, the light out. Nita for a time sat next to me, but as it grew dusky she took off her dress and saddle shoes, went to the bed, and leaned back against the iron headboard, which was cushioned partly by a lumpy pillow whose striped gray-and-white ticking showed through the damp pillowcase. Once the mosquitoes, light or no light, thickened in the dark, I went inside and checked the two window screens and settled down alongside Nita. We sat propped up, staring at the window opposite the foot of the bed, where now and then a light showed as a car passed into town. During an hour only one headlight bored eastward toward the Salton Sea.

"Is it the way to Las Vegas?"

"Not really."

"What was he doing here?"

"I looked at the map in the gas station. Spider should have gone to San Bernardino the way we came on the bus, then to Barstow and into Nevada. I don't know. Maybe he wanted to see Palm Springs. Or the Indian country near here."

"He didn't tell me that."

"What did he say?"

"He said his brother that's the next youngest one found a job on the Boulder Dam and was going to meet him in Las Vegas."

"He could have read a map wrong."

"No. Since he's had the Harley he would read maps and tell me how to get from one place to another—places we even didn't want to go to."

"Maybe he called the brother at the last minute to meet him here."

"Spider wouldn't. He never used the phone."

"Nita, he didn't stop in Indio. I didn't tell you before, but the police checked the tourist homes and cabins to look for his belongings."

"So, where was he going?"

"He was hit going out of town on Route 60, on the road to Phoenix. Spider just sort of drifted right into the car at the last minute, the police said. I asked if the Harley skittered out of a soft spot in the road—the sun boils the road out here—but the police said the driver of the car claimed not, and they believed him."

"Oh, God. God damn it. Spider died in a place where he wasn't supposed to be. Was he afraid? Was he running away? He wasn't lost."

I had already asked myself the same questions and I suppose it was helplessness that caused me to say, "He didn't suffer, anyhow."

"Johnny." She was crying now, her eyes wide open. "What's that got to do with it? People always say it's a blessing to die quick. Whose blessing?"

"Maybe it hurts, Nita, but it's true that what happens to you is like yourself. I mean that Spider never was going anywhere special, or particular."

"I asked him."

"What? You mean, about coming to California?"

Nita took her slip off; she did it by folds because it was soaking wet. She dropped it at the side of the bed, crossed her brassiere with one arm while she arched the other over her still smooth hair. "Yes. I asked him. When I met Spider, he'd left his folks' farm to look for a job in our hometown. I was leaving home that same day; it was the saint's day. He offered to buy me an Eskimo Pie and we started talking. I asked him all of a sudden, 'You want to go to California?' And he answered, 'I might as well.' But I didn't let it go at that. I told Spider to decide on his own. 'This is no army hitch,' I told him. 'I might pull out of L.A. the day after I get there.' And he made it firm he really wanted to go, saying he wouldn't be 'no bother.' "

"And he wasn't?"

"Everybody's a bother. You know that. If you like somebody, you put up with it."

"And is it the same if you love somebody?"

"I don't know. I've never been in love. Spider knew that, but it didn't make any difference to him so long as we were together. At first we weren't even together. We went out to L.A. and stayed in a rooming house at South Gate for about three weeks before we went to the island. We didn't move into the same room until we came to the Greek's."

The air cooled a bit when it became darker in the room than outside: the window framed the difference. I didn't say anything for a long time.

"What are you thinking, Johnny? It's your getting him the Harley, isn't it?"

"That's got nothing to do with it."

"Yes, it does. I think everything has got to do with it, whether you give somebody a thing, or keep it away from them. We all changed Spider. It was just part of it, your helping him buy the cycle. Spider told me he'd never met anyone like you, John."

98

I lit a cigaret and gave it to Nita, and lit another for myself. She drew deeply and mixed spumes of smoke with her words. "You're having trouble with that, aren't you? You and Spider weren't friends. Probably you don't know that, but he did. He wasn't stupid."

"It was nothing to do with him. I never counted on what he knew, or didn't know."

"Spider understood you have a good heart about poor people, like Eleanor Roosevelt. But, Johnny, you're not cut out to take people the way they are. You're always looking for some kind of identification. Like a G-man."

"That's not fair, Nita. I never looked down on Spider."

"No, you wouldn't. You would have wanted Spider to stand for something." She sat higher on the bed, her knees up and her heels tacked against her thighs. I thought this a gesture of revived energy, but in her eyes I could see, from the little light left, the sleeplessness of two days overtaking her. "Johnny, why should I tell you how you act?"

"I don't know. I never know what it is people want, I guess. I asked Spider that question once."

"What did he say?"

"He said he wanted you to get what you want. But he didn't know what it was."

"No."

"Well, it's not hard," I said. "Everybody is supposed to want to be happy."

"Maybe. I want to be busy. I should have told Spider that."

"You would have ended up making plans if you had. Nita, you don't want plans. Isn't that why you came to California? Quick moves."

"God damn it," she said slowly, sliding down on the

headboard so that her head was bent toward her raised-up knees, crouching to sleep. "I stayed with Spider because he didn't ask anything. Dolores says that I did."

"Poor Spider," I said, lighting another cigaret. "He didn't deserve it."

"Nobody deserves," Nita said in a slurring whisper. She was asleep.

Chapter

9

Nita came back two days later, but I did not see her right away because she moved out of the Greek's. This surprised some of the regulars until they concluded by consensus that she would not stay where painful reminiscences remained. But I was not surprised. That night in Indio, as I sat smoking through the night next to a sleeping Nita, I was inclined to accept that she would proceed whole from event to event, without calculation but surely. Spider's death, whatever else it meant to Nita, she would understand at once as releasing her and impelling her. In those days when I was her volleyball teammate or when we gossiped aimlessly in the print shop, it was improbable to think that one day her native wit and quickness could gain her a career, that she could be sought after and perhaps feared. It didn't seem improbable now. She might already have made that kind of mark.

Nothing much was said about Spider the first or second day I was back, possibly because it was hard for some of the Greek's roomers to recall anything he had done, or even where he was from. In the end it was the Harley-Davidson that distinguished him. There grew the legend that Spider met death in a glorious burst of inept daring. It was reported that on a narrow road he had come upon the headlights of a Pierce-Arrow—these are shaped like cornucopias and set wide apart on the fenders of that huge car—and having mistaken these for the headlights of two approaching motorcycles, Spider dashed between them. I didn't deny the story. It would only have diminished Spider's small legacy.

I told Leonid about the death of Spider when I repaid him the loan; he had already learned of it by asking others how I had so enraged Sergio. He did not remain interested except for the information that I had spent so much time in the company of Nita. "You going to be careful, Johnny?" I thought he spoke of motorcycles, but it was women. He went on: "I worry about yellow pretty girl. Her husband, I know his personality. A peasant. A little drunk and he will beat her." When I told Leonid that I would not allow that, he said that there were only two choices. You could either humiliate the husband until he took some foolish action, or else take his wife away. "It's not like betting horses, Johnny," Leonid summarized. "Everybody can lose."

Sergio did not dock my pay for being AWOL and uncharacteristically did not speak of it. Of course, I was busy. The hotel was still full although the children's dining room was closed and most families had left on the wane of the season. I saw Jean in the kitchen immediately on my return and persuaded her to meet me in the unused employment office to tell her of the trip to Indio. She asked if Nita suffered badly. I insisted on telling her of the long hot night, asking what she made of Nita's closing so abruptly the question of just what Spider was doing at Indio. She thought it odd but not mysterious and was more concerned that Nita had to wait to meet relatives who would not accept her connection to Spider.

"Especially," I said, "if they happened to find out that Nita and I spent the night together." I looked at Jean seriously. "Nothing happened."

"Yes, I know that. With you it would be important."

"And with you?"

"It's important for me, too," she whispered, reaching up to kiss my ear. She laughed later when I asked her to ride the ferry for an hour that afternoon. "We're beginning to count ships like kids counting station-wagon cars on a street. Did you ever count with another kid by wetting your thumb and stamping your palm with your fist?"

"Sure. But in California you are backward. We counted Cords and Duesenbergs instead of station wagons."

Come to think of it, Jean was right about the ships: there were more and more of them at anchor in the bay or tied at the bases, destroyers and destroyer escorts, tenders and supply ships, and, at one time, two cruisers. Jean said her father at Pearl Harbor was seeing more ships, allowing that it was in the same ocean.

Whenever Jean raised the question of the war in Europe, she told me that I was curiously detached. Despite my sharing in some part my father's concern over the Axis conquest of Yugoslavia just five months before, she was right about me. The isolationist politics of the West was so pervasive that it made the war in Europe appear unattached to ordinary possibilities. I remember a year before the fall of Belgrade, in April of 1940, regarding myself as disinterested as I sat in university drugstores looking at maps in *Time* with their red sweeping arrows marking the attack on Norway and showing the sea race called Skagerrak. It struck me as perverse, but not shameful, that I didn't feel great compassion for the defeated or a fearful alarm over the victors, especially as I expected to be enlisted in the war if it spread and found the prospect not at all threatening. But then, Disraeli said no young man really expects to die.

Jean knew of my repeated talks with a rich old man who was one of my regular numbers on the room-service callboard. He began to feign a physical indisposition at lunchtime so that I would serve him in his room and thus continue the dialog we began by chance one morning. I talked of the war with him impersonally, though hardly unintellectually, for his passion was geopolitics. He had been a wildcatter in the Kern River Field at Bakersfield before the Great War and in 1928 had sold his holdings to Associated Oil Company. He lived year round at the hotel, having given up a large house on the island when his wife died. Now he did little more than look after his investments—stopping in the lobby twice a day to read the ticker and once or twice a week to call New York before the market closed—and read books of history and prophecy on nations and empires. "Current events," he told me, "are inclinations enacted."

The oilman was the guest I talked books with seriously, he and the precisely mannered widow of the Santa Fe treasurer, who was solely given to reading fiction and, at that, narrowly devoted to Ellen Glasgow and Willa Cather and Kathleen Norris. ("Admit it," she said to me once. "You are a snob and have only read Frank, not Kathleen, of the Norrises.") I could have readily approached, and now regret that I did not, the refugee sisters as they sat reading Mann and Werfel in German editions in the sunroom. The widow pressed Willa Cather's novels on me, and I accepted them though I dared not admit to reading hardly at all that summer. Rashly I had told her the Cather stories were better than the novels for being not so full of philosophical embroidery. "Embroidery!" she gasped. "What can you be doing, speaking of appliqué? Miss Cather is, if anything, a weaver and what her characters think is whole cloth with what they are and do." I was impressed by that long and consistent metaphor, but I knew, guiltily, that I was more likely at present to spend time at the Greek's table than the Archbishop's.

As for the old man, he was at that time reading Hector Bolitho, Philip Guedalla, Arnold Toynbee, and John Strachey. But it was not of authors that we talked; rather, of historical interpretations, political probabilities, military strategies. He had no doubt whatever that war would come to the United States within eight months—"in the spring in Europe, when the ice melts; anytime in the Pacific, where there's damn little ice to worry about." He pressed me on this. "How is it that you young guys never talk about the war?"

"We don't?"

"By Christ, you don't. Half this country won't admit there's a war going on."

"Which half? Young or old? Rich or poor?"

"That, too, I guess, but I'm talking, as you know well, about East and West."

"It's called isolationism. 'Burton K. Wheeler speaks here tonight!' "

"You know your college friend who works in the bar? When I told him that Rommel might cork up the Mediterranean, he asked if Rommel was an admiral."

I smiled. "That's called uninformed isolationism."

Yet he was not really interested in public opinion, however instructed, for he believed that it was not contemporary exercise of power but, rather, geopolitics that decided war; and this is the province of theorists and historians as much as it is of officials and partisans. He quoted Spengler and Admiral Mahan and especially Mackinder, whose theory of an Asian "heartland" he accepted generally. I argued that America—which the old man believed, along with Henry Adams, to be the empire of the twentieth century—didn't fit the heartland hypothesis convincingly.

"That's not the whole of it," he replied, biting his Havana cigar (occasionally he offered me one, which I would subsequently take to Leonid or Harry). I sat smoking a cigaret at the luncheon table I'd just laid for him. "No. No. I don't believe that empires start in continental centers. They are placed on the edges of continents. True, they spread out from those edges, but they don't generally have too big a center to defend—or retreat to."

"The Greeks and Romans, yes," I agreed.

"And the Moors and the Spanish and the British."

"Okay," I said. "It works, but not all the time. The Germans aren't on the edge."

"Of course not. They're on the indefensible flat plain that runs from Paris to Moscow. What Hitler wants, in fact, to do is to get to the edges, to the Black Sea, the Mediterranean, to the Pacific possibly."

I was still fighting. "It doesn't explain the United States, which has a center and edges both and is an empire of sorts. Or it doesn't explain China's having a center and edges and not being properly an empire."

"That's where this war—the one that nobody notices—comes in," he said. "The Japs are an empire and a hungry one, all edges and no center."

Without leaving geopolitics, the old man and I got on to smaller game, civil wars. I cannot remember which of us—it must have been he—began to tinker with the notion that the most persistent or vicious colonial wars occur on peninsulas. We traded names like baseball cards. Greece (Athens and Sparta, Macedon and Thebes). Shantung (Chinese versus Russians, Germans and British versus Chinese, Japanese versus Chinese). Spain (Spaniards versus Moors, Hapsburgs versus Bourbons, Republicans versus Nationalists). Korea (Chinese versus Japanese). Jutland and Indochina and on and on into the encyclopedia that he bought just for this purpose. I claimed a foul when I discovered his encyclopedia.

I suppose I reported the sessions with the old man too triumphantly to Jean. She grew distracted as she listened and finally was angered as we lay between the Navy blankets on the beach. Her skin was still moist as she looked down at me. Sweat hung like cheap glass beads from her marvelous breasts. I kissed her eyes and tasted salt.

"What's wrong?"

"It's not just a game, war."

"Well, I didn't say that. It's a talking contest between the old man and me."

"What about the rest of us? You'll go and I'll go. Everything will change." She lay back. We stared at the sandpipers picking minute leftovers from the sea's retreat.

"I'm not going anywhere tomorrow, for God's sake. Whatever the old man says, wars start when you have something to fight them against—or with. The Americans don't have a single soldier stationed in Europe." This argument was plainly devious, for the Great War started for the United States without troops in France, yet I was not prepared for Jean's rebuttal.

"We've got soldiers and sailors in the Pacific. My dad is there."

"You're right. But the war's already been going on two years and we're not in. It's more likely that instead of fighting, Americans will get rich from supplying both sides."

"Is that the way it ends?" she asked tartly. "Making money?"

"No, of course not. Listen, Jeannie, we're not even talking about you and me. The old man and I are arguing over history. He's a pretty cynical old guy. He thinks history is just one life strung out after another, people end to end."

"And what do you think?"

"I think history is either absurd or misplayed, a story that can't be finished."

She looked at me, her eyes filled, and said, "There is nothing wrong with that. Fairy tales aren't finished." Before I dropped her off about north of her house, we did not speak again. Dressing and leaving our spot on the beach below the road, each of us was pointedly busy.

"Shall we still go to Los Angeles?" I reached over to unlatch her side of the car.

"If you want."

"For Christ sake, Jean."

She surprised me. "No, for my sake. Let's go."

Two days later, a Wednesday, we went ahead with a plan that had been rehearsed weeks before, before Indio. Jean would plead the need to see her mother at Compton. I suggested she say her mother was ailing, but Jean disagreed. She was herself habitually truthful, but I think she knew, as a victim, that liars ought not to be too literal. I would take my normal day off plus an extra—paying

Shosh to fill in for me a second day if it coincided with his own time off—and risking Sergio's reprisal, I'd cadge a third day. Actually, I first proposed this tryst after I won the big game and told Jean that we could stay at either the Huntington or the Beverly Wilshire. She was so delighted that she kept saying, "It won't happen! I can't deserve it, but I'll take it." She had never stayed in a hotel. On her honeymoon she and George had rented a cabin near Oceanside.

We settled for less luxury because I couldn't manage the extra day from Shosh. We went no farther than La Jolla, which we reached rather grandly by train, getting off nine miles away—La Jolla is San Diego's Back Bay or Pasadena, its first and fashionable railway stop. We checked into the Del Charro Hotel and found we were nondescript like the other guests, not idle or purposeful. We walked in the bright sunshine both mornings, made love over the luncheon hour, and went out walking again until we found an expensive place where we could eat and talk for two or three hours.

Jean laid plans during the short train ride: the first day we'd stick to the shore, the second to the town. We walked down the narrow streets winding to the sea where higher up the red-tiled houses showed elephant palms in spacious yards. Closer to the shore, the older and smaller houses settled for less; lilac bushes leaned against faded stucco and warped shingles. We sat on the sea wall above La Jolla Cove, which was like a pirate movie set: a semicircle carved out of the cliff, firs and cypresses ringing the top; a beige beach was protected by arms of the cove, the left one pitted with grottoes where eddies linger, the right with rock shale layered like slabs of shiny horn. A hundred yards from the cove were single rocks that looked as if they had strayed toward shore carrying crowns of guano left by cormorants and gulls and loons. Brown pelicans trolled overhead.

It is not the dimming distance, not the willful obscurantism of memory that makes me uncertain whether I ever held hope that our departing the island on this occasion would decide us to keep going, leaving for good together. Jean was at times during the two days grave and intent, but she did not seem to prefigure. I myself knew that fifteen hundred dollars could probably see Jean and me through a six-week waiting period for her to gain a Nevada divorce. I happened on this information by listening to Nita's account of how she was once paid eight dollars a time to sit as a shill for two or three hours at various twenty-one and roulette tables in Reno gambling houses. She had stopped in Reno the first time she came to California and found that being hired by the house to gamble, so as to make a table look busy and tempting to undecisive customers, was a favorite temporary profession of women who were waiting out their divorce decrees. Twelve to fifteen hundred dollars freed some of these women, Nita said.

Nothing like this was intimated as we walked the streets of downtown La Jolla playing hooky. We set free helium balloons on Silverado Street near the Arcade, with its mission bell hanging over an entrance to nothing more than another street, and watched them disappear over the hills to the east. The second afternoon we sought places that would, I think now, fix our attention and not let our thoughts run to the end. Jean found cupolas and domes she called "Easter eggs," brightly enameled shells with vaguely Moorish geometric designs. One of these topped an architectural marvel, a building with a ribbed fan placed over two delicate fluted pilasters between which there was a bluntly painted black-and-white sign that said METHODIST CHURCH. We sat under the grape trellis running away from the church and ate tangerines we'd bought in the Arcade. "This is called adventure," I told Jean when she said it was strange sitting here, not being something else, doing whatever else.

"It isn't dangerous," Jean replied.

"No. It's just a kind of chance." Try as I might, I could not help thinking right then that by loving someone you removed a part of chance from your life. Not even a woman's devotion would exonerate her of that. And a man's fidelity might remind her of it. I kissed Jean under the grape trellis, drew away and said, "I love you." She replied, "Thank you."

The next morning at seven o'clock we caught a bus for downtown San Diego, making it necessary for Jean to wait there until eleven, when she could properly return to the island as if she'd come down on the early-morning train from Los Angeles.

I reported to work after stopping at my room. It was the first week of September, the last days in the decrement of the summer season. At the Greek's there were signs of winding down. Most of the college students who lived in the north had gone earlier, leaving the beachcomber boys who worked occasionally in the store and stayed in the rooms above only when they were not on surfing picnics up and down the coast. Now they, too, were gone, some to re-enter or begin college; two of them had gone to Yuma in hope of signing on as extras on movie locations. Shosh was leaving for Los Angeles on the prospect of a job from Elsa Lanchester. He told me it was on La Cienega Boulevard, recently opened, a two-way theater in a hall fitted with rattan streetcar seats that could be faced one way for the audience to watch a puppet show and then turned the other way for them to watch live actors, of whom Miss Lanchester was the star. Shosh had met her the year before at the Pasadena Playhouse. He stopped by to see me the night after I returned, just as I had sat down at a card game. I quit after playing two hands and bought Shosh a beer and walked him down the street to the corner. He was going to the hotel dormitory, where he'd stayed the last few weeks to save money for what he called his "road-company clothes."

"This has been," he said when we stopped, "what is called a fast study. An actor observes people, you know; that's what we do, observe people. But I can't say, Big John, as they call you, that observing you has done me a bit of good."

"Does that mean I'm unique, incomparable?"

"I don't know how long it will last: probably the next time, you'll be like everybody else."

"Probably."

"But I'll read about you one day. One way or another, Big John, you're not going to settle."

"Neither will you, Shosh."

"No, I don't want to, but I just might end up being eccentric instead of successful."

"In the movies you can be both."

"Jesus, you're right. I wonder why I don't think of things like that?" He feigned a punch toward my middle.

"Well." We seemed to amble without moving.

"Well, nothing. I've got to go. You want to get back and make some more money, which I don't blame you for after the killing you made at the Greek's. Which also reminds me: can you lend me a ten-spot?"

"I can."

"Just give me the ten, John. Don't lend it. I don't want to feel cunning."

"You're in luck," I said, giving him two fives.

"Yeah. Don't bet on it." He turned the corner, walking away fast, as he always did. I went back to the Greek's.

Chapter

10

At the table were seven players—my chair was now occupied by Jackson—playing dealer's choice, draw or stud, with a five-dollar ante and twenty-five-dollar limit. The Greek was playing; also the retired captain, the garageman from the spit, a couple of car dealers from Phoenix who were attending a convention at the U.S. Grant Hotel in San Diego, and the Armenian fruit dealer whom the Greek visited every afternoon. I watched them from a high-backed stool, smoking, not particularly eager to rejoin the game. Dolores sat behind the players' circle and took up the house's share of the pot each hand by leaning forward. From across the way I kept noticing how the top curves of her breasts touched. She looked up once and smiled and I remembered when she said that learning her name was of no value to me.

"Rumpelstiltskin," I said to Dolores suddenly. Jackson looked around and said, "If that's your best snappy dialog, you can have your chair back. I'm tapped out." The first six or seven hands were not much, none taking a pot with better than kings, three of a kind. I didn't stay in long enough to call any of them. The Armenian and the captain once or twice, I noticed, drew on a low pair hoping to catch a third, but neither tried to bluff on his hopes. The Greek bluffed on one hand that he won with only three sixes—these he showed as openers. He had asked for only one card on discarding, thereby convincing one of the Phoenix players not to pay in fifty-five dollars to call when in fact he could have beaten the Greek with three eights. He showed these in disgust, admitting he had assumed the Greek had drawn a full house after opening on two pairs.

Each of the Phoenix car dealers kept about five hundred dollars in chips and bills before him. The second one got beyond one thousand before he dropped six hundred on one hand when he bet a full house against the captain's own full house, three tens losing to three jacks. I played with two hundred dollars as my table stake and ran it up and down for more than an hour, never reaching past four hundred and fifty. The Greek played modestly except for the one hand when he bluffed. There wasn't a lot of action; the hands were not building.

The second time the deal came to me I chose to play stud and asked for a new deck, a privilege accorded if you threw a five-dollar chip to the house. I slit open the end of the cellophane, shuffled, and offered the captain the cut, which he declined with a head shake. I dealt round the hole cards, then the up cards: "Seven and a nine and a queen and a four and a jack and a trey and the dealer is high with the ace. I bet twenty-five dollars. You're under the gun, Captain." The captain folded his seven, as did the garageman his nine. The Greek with his queen stayed and raised twenty-five. The Armenian folded, no doubt on the sound injunction to quit if you are beaten on the board not just once but twice. One of the Phoenix men—the one who lost the big pot—folded with a jack; but the other one stayed with his trey, and I figured he had drawn a pair. As I myself held a pair with an ace in the hole, my problem at this stage was to hold open the game to gain a bigger pot. In stud a pair of aces can of course be bested readily, but when only one or two cards have been played, an ace showing makes some players drop early. I paid in twenty-five but did not raise. There were three of us left.

I dealt the Greek a second queen, the Phoenix man got an ace of hearts, and for myself I turned up a ten. The Greek looked down at my hand, an ace of spades and a ten showing, and said, "Twenty-five." Obviously he was not ignoring the other hand's ace. Surprisingly and foolishly, the Phoenix man stayed. His pair of treys, if indeed he had them, could not after all beat either the Greek's pair of queens showing or, for all he knew, my own pair of aces or pair of tens. Anyway, he paid twenty-five and I paid and raised another twenty-five, as did the Greek, twenty-five and twenty-five. Now our opponent folded, muttering that sometimes he had "more dollars than sense." I raised another twenty-five, which the Greek met but didn't increase, looking at me across a spray of Bakelite blue and red chips. Behind me, Jackson whistled and said to no one in particular, "Already too many for tiddlywinks."

I dealt the Greek another queen, the third one showing, and dropped on my own hand my third ace, two up and one down. And there it was. The Greek was looking down at his three queens, and across the table, at my two aces and a ten. On the board the Greek had me beaten, but I was convinced that at this point I had him. Nothing was notable in his face except that the pouches under his eyes had darkened; when he leaned back out of the circle of light they were almost black. I looked at Dolores, now standing directly behind him, but she turned her eyes down.

"It's your bet, Greek," I said.

"I know."

"What is it? What, then?"

"You want to raise a bigger roll?" he replied. "Is that it?" I thought I heard a feint in his voice. My excitement made me search for signs.

"Are we sticking with the twenty-five-dollar limit?" I countered.

The Greek said, deliberately, "No, it's okay; if you want, we'll play table stakes." His left hand settled on a neat pile of twenty- and fifty-dollar bills, the diamond on his index finger catching the light. For some reason, I'd never noticed before that the diamonds on his hand were matched, like cuff links. "I got about two thousand here. If you want to play table stakes, I give you fifteen minutes to get up a roll."

"I can."

"I know you can. But if you want to play, then I'll bet. How much you got there? I bet whatever you got." The Greek's voice held the intimation of climax.

Now there were more than a dozen people surrounding the table. I pushed back my chair and as I rose I saw Dolores's eyes, strained wide, her slightly parted Clara Bow lips. She shook her head, I thought, but then decided not.

"Are you playing?"

"Take it easy. Three hundred eighty," I said, pushing the remaining chips and all the bills before me to the center. After he matched the amount, I said, "I'll be back." I went out into the street, up the staircase to my room, where I dug out from a locked portable-typewriter case thirteen one-hundred-dollar bills and two fifties. I folded these into my front pants pocket and went downstairs, having been away four or five minutes, to discover that there were more than twenty people in a cluster at the poker table. I saw immediately that the captain had left the store, Jackson claiming his chair, the others sitting as before.

"You ready?" the Greek asked. "The cards don't get better with age."

Picking up the deck, I felt its diminished weight; more than a third of the cards were set before me and the Greek or lay discarded. Dealing, I felt as if I were coming down a fast elevator. The Greek's card sailed precisely, so that it fell just short of his hand. It was a nine of clubs. He now had showing the new nine, a queen of spades, a queen of clubs, a queen of diamonds. The Greek barely looked down. I dealt myself a ten of diamonds. Before me lay the new ten, the second ten, clubs, the ace of spades, the ace of clubs. My down card, the ace of diamonds, gave a three-ace-high full house. On the face the Greek was a winner, his three queens showing against my two tens and two aces.

He said, "The spots don't change while we look at them." I didn't answer. "I bet your whole roll. What is it, John?"

"I've got fourteen hundred dollars here."

"Okay. Fourteen it is. You can call." He stacked bills and moved them toward the center. Next to me, Jackson said, "You got to figure your own investment up to now, not the whole pot." This seemed to penetrate the Greek's stolidness, for he looked at Jackson scornfully and said,

"He can count, like all you college guys."

If I was not listening it was because I was fixed by the notion that there was little to think about. I looked intently, but not to concentrate, at the sheaf of bills splayed against the chips and the baize. I wished there was a complication, a larger equation, with coefficients, so that I could deliberate on the "X" that lay face down before the Greek. He was either betting that he held a winning full house, his three queens ranking my three tens, mistaking my three of a kind as tens, or else he was bluffing against my insecurity, knowing that a loss could wipe out my whole summer and could even make me leave the island in the confusion of debt. But he couldn't beat me with a full house, as I so securely knew, so the only possibility meaningful to me was that he held downside the fourth queen.

I never bet on statistical odds except for simple ones that attach to the chances of drawing a third card to a pair or filling an open-ended flush or straight. On big hands, four of a kind and straight flushes, the odds rise to such heights that they overwhelm your judgment rather than inform it. I knew that the fourth queen had not been dealt to any hand face up; in the intensity of the moment I did remember then that the odds against drawing four of a kind are almost five thousand to one. But I took no consolation from this because I also was aware that hands can be won, are won, with straight flushes, where the odds are at least fifty thousand to one. How long this contemplation lasted I have no idea. The only sound was matches struck. I looked at the Greek's hands. They were steady, but then, his wrists were stayed by the edge of the table. I waited. But I knew from the first that I would shove my stack of bills out. When I did, it felt conventional.

The Greek turned over his hole card. It was the queen of hearts, the fourth queen.

I stood up and walked away, down the one step to the front of the store and out the door. That night the new moon left the streets dark. I walked briskly, as if I had an appointment, toward the boulevard and westward to the Carnegie Library, where I mounted the steps and sat with my back against the brass bossed door, smoking and looking onto the double roadway, where the street lamps spotted on the pavement targets of light. I sat a long time, until the fog lowered and the frosted globes of the street lamps lost their outlines and became attenuated, like candles. There was no wind. The streetcars had stopped running. I felt as if I were wasted in this place just by being sentient.

"Big Johnny?" Nita whispered against the panel of her door on the second floor above the print shop.

"Yes."

"Has something gone wrong?"

"No."

"What is it?"

"Open the door, Nita, for Pete's sake! I'm not collecting for the Red Cross."

She stood back from the door as I came through, minding that it didn't pinch her small brown feet. She wore as a nightgown a cotton wraparound dress, the kind that waitresses wear as uniforms. I don't think she had anything on underneath. She stood still while I went to the window, staring out aimlessly, and looked back. I had not before seen her room. It was neatly kept: twin beds, twin bureaus, a Pullman kitchen closed off from the bedroom by a chenille curtain that hung from gold-painted wooden rings.

"You want some coffee?"

"I haven't been drinking."

"I didn't think you had. But it's almost breakfast. Some people drink coffee for breakfast."

"Okay. Okay. Can I lie down?" I lay on the bed that was made, cradling my head on the palms of my hands, exhaling smoke toward the ceiling. Nita put a percolator on a little two-burner stove and after a while put down a coffee mug and a nut-and-raisin bun on the table between the beds. She sat on the other bed, then pulled the blanket up to cover her feet.

"Can I ask any questions?"

"You can. I would if somebody came calling at four or five in the morning."

"Is it Jean?"

I started. "What do you mean? What about Jean?"

"Now, let's not be doing that. Everybody knows about you and Jean. Well, not everybody. If her husband knew, you'd hear from him."

"No, it's not Jean. It was a card game."

"At the Greek's? Who was there?"

"Me and the Greek and two car dealers staying in San Diego, and the garageman and the captain and the Greek's Armenian friend. Jackson played only a little bit. I took his place when I came back from saying good-bye to Shosh."

"I know. Shosh stopped by to borrow ten dollars off me."

"You, too. He's a bad actor. I don't mean on the stage. This coffee is a little thin, Nita."

"Isn't it, though? I only had enough for one. I wasn't counting on company tonight." I stared at the cracks in the ceiling, not thinking about anything, peering at the outlines of hands, noses, handles, cups, knives made by cracks in the plaster. I must have dozed, for I heard Nita's voice approaching.

"You lost, didn't you?"

"Yes. I lost to the Greek. I lost every damn dollar I had."

"How much?"

"There was more than four thousand dollars in the pot, about nineteen hundred of it mine."

"What?"

"He took it all on one hand with four queens. Can you believe that? Four queens."

Nita unlaced my shoes, let them drop at the end of the bed, and brought over from a maplewood armchair a Navaho blanket with a terrible design and ran it up from my feet to my chest. She yawned, clasped her mouth with a feigned gesture of shock, and leaned over and kissed me on the bridge of my nose.

"I don't want to sleep," I said wearily to her. "I'd better go."

"No, Johnny, you want to sleep, and right now you haven't got anyplace to go. I'll wake you about seven so you can go to work."

"I'm not tired, Nita. I feel like a damn fool."

"I won't take that away from you. You had no cause to take the Greek on. He's been waiting for the chance to hurt you, waiting a long time."

"I don't see that. I told you once I never argued with him."

"Jesus, Johnny, he didn't want to argue with you. He wanted to beat you."

"That's poker."

"No. That's Dolores."

I looked at her curiously, as if a third person had entered the room without our being warned of it. "You've got that wrong, Nita. I had nothing to do with Dolores. We never talked anytime longer than two minutes, tops."

"You think the Greek hasn't seen her look at you? Light a match to her and she'd go off. Whoosh!"

I couldn't reply. It was somehow unconnected, all this.

"Johnny, when some girl finally chooses you, you won't even know it."

"Is it that bad?"

"No. I just hope she won't give you trouble."

"I've got enough of that now. I'm broke."

"It makes me sick. How did you lose, really?"

"I thought the Greek was bluffing, only he wasn't."

"It figures," Nita said, drawing deeply on her cigaret in reflection. "He wouldn't want to trick you. He'd want to beat you in the open. He'd want to be damn, dead sure."

I started to yawn and then fought it back, making a grimace. I barely heard Nita when she said, "Go to sleep. We're sleeping like brother and sister in towns you won't remember the names of someday."

When I next thought about myself it was morning, only a couple of hours later. Nita was asleep in the other bed and her alarm clock on the bureau read a few minutes before seven. I went over and turned off the alarm switch and went downstairs to the street to a dinette next door to the print shop. When it opened at seven I had coffee and, finding myself hungry, ate three orders of easy-over eggs and bacon. It wasn't until I lit my first cigaret that the ache of my loss surged. I felt as if I had mislaid the money, that it was recoverable only by accident and not by me, that it was missing in an inexcusable way, like an old woman's savings left on a streetcar in a paper bag. I did not feel anger, certainly none toward the Greek, nor did

123

I conceive that some arcane fault of mine had acted to make me lose the whole summer's pay and my chance— though I was not quite sure how—to make emphatic my feeling for Jean. I did not even feel unlucky, probably because I know that every card played, every pair of dice rolled, is one act in a long and putatively infinite series: nobody's fate is settled in a stroke, for everything is in motion and is alike, a series of one.

Chapter

11

By the time I reached the hotel I was forced to consider how my loss must appear to some others, for whom it would be vicariously momentous. It was seven-fifty when I went into the kitchen. Jean was not there because today was not her early shift, but Leon was on hand to offer me a croissant to go with the coffee that I took simply not to change my routine.

He started right in with the news. The San Diego morning paper put the German advance into eastern Ukrainia, the mechanized divisions of the Wehrmacht ready to form a pincer, an arc pointed at Moscow on the north and at Volvograd on the south. Just over twenty years before, Leonid had fought with foreign forces, the Czechs, against Communist Russians he then accused of seizing his homeland; now it was being defended by the same Communists against other foreigners. Irony is so common that it is a wonder that it is remarked at all. I told Father Oliver, when we once talked of George Bernard Shaw's plays, that irony is the evolving discovery of the known between enemies or friends, either one, it scarcely makes any difference. Historians are ironists by trade, readers of the past who have peeked at the next chapter. But it seemed a long time ago that I talked with Father Oliver, and then speculation was not costly, not touching on whole peoples. I told Leon that we'd talk later, after I had a chance to read the papers. I went off to begin the breakfast rounds.

After three trips up the staircases and around the galleries above the empty patio, I came down into the room-service room to discover that the news was out. Two old hands took up the banter, tossing it back and forth like a softball: "I've heard of shills spending twenty bucks, but imagine a guy spending two thousand of his own money to advertise the Greek's game. Your trouble, Big John, is that in college they don't teach four is bigger than five." I was not in the least tempted to reply, but also I did not trust myself to stay in the room too long. Soon someone would press to bring the repartee to a climax and would command my response, which could be no less than to punch somebody. I took a number out of sequence to no one's objection and went upstairs, where I was glad to be hailed by the old wildcatter, who stood outside his suite looking impatient—as if I were late for an appointment.

"Have you got a minute? Of course you haven't. Take one anyway, unless you're carrying something that will turn bitterly cold." I put down my heater outside his door and went in to take a seat at the huge glass-topped table he had installed himself. On it the silver coffee Thermos with a stopper was probably the oldest object in the sitting room. The old man, though a year-round resident, managed to appear actively impermanent. "You remember what we were talking about?" he asked.

"Money, power, war, honor. What was it? Is there anything else to talk about?"

He grinned. "That's about it: most things are off the point."

"I know what's happened. You've thought of a rebuttal to whatever I said last."

"Right. You said the United States doesn't fit the 'edges' theory. I've decided that that's directly because of the decline of sea travel and rise of air power. In the future, empires won't start or stay on the edges. They will be land masses with centers. The United States is one such."

"What else does that leave?"

"Russia and China."

"It's strange. We're up here talking about Russia as a future empire, yet just an hour ago I was consoling my Russian friend in the kitchen about the defeat of the Russians by the Wehrmacht."

"Not so strange. This is nineteen forty-one. I'm talking about ten or twenty years from now."

"That assumes the Germans will fail."

"Of course. Once they stop moving, they're dead. Haven't you been following my lectures?"

"What does it all prove, then?"

"I doubt it proves anything," the old man said, reverting to his sly agnosticism. "Some possibilities become facts."

I smiled, surprised that I felt lightened in spirit, and said to him, "I'll buy it. Don't bother to wrap it."

"Not so fast," he said. "I'm sure I left something out. You'll be up here in a couple of days to say what I left out —probably India or Brazil."

"Probably. You want me to take these cups?"

"No, let them be. No point in breaking another fellow's rice bowl."

As I left his room and walked along the fourth-floor

corridor, I peered down at the change of light caused by small low clouds stalled in the morning sky. Then I saw someone running into the patio from the main entrance. Unmistakably it was Jean, though she was not wearing her white kitchen uniform, and the usual supple motion of her stride was eccentrically interrupted by her holding her cheek, one elbow stuck straight out. I called down to her. She looked behind her first, then waved at me: "Johnny! My God! Don't come down." Before I could reply she had run to the stairwell on my side and started up the stairs. I dropped the heater and ran down until we met at the second landing, Jean falling against me, locking her hands behind me and sobbing hard. As I bent over to kiss the fine blond hair on her neck, I saw blood on my jacket. First I thought of dabbing her cheek with a handkerchief, but she would not let go of me. Slowly her gasping subsided.

"It's George. My God."

"Where is he?"

"He's looking for you: he's got a gun."

"How do you know?" Looking at her bleeding face, I thought it a graceless, if practical, question.

"He found out about us just this morning."

"How? Did he hit you right then?"

"You know the man who runs the garage?" She held her breath to steady her voice. "He told Elmore when he stopped by this morning to get gas that you had lost all your money playing poker."

"I did, Jean. But what has that to do with it?"

"He told Elmore that he figured that George could relax now, something like that, because you were broke and couldn't go anywhere with me."

"The bastard. I've played cards with him a dozen times and I never mentioned you or George or his folks."

"Elmore drove back to the house—he didn't go to work —and told George. George yelled and ran around the house, arguing with his mother and dad. He slapped me a couple of times; then he went out and sat for a long time in back, staring at the bay. Finally, he went into the garage and got a revolver he hides in the car. I ran out to try to stop him and that's when he waved me back with the gun—the part that sticks up at the end scraped my face."

"Oh, Jesus, Jean. What I've done to you!"

"You didn't do it. You've got to go before George finds you."

"Does he know you're here?"

"No. After he drove off, I took Elmore's car and followed him. I came up the back way from the employment office. George was in the kitchen asking Leon about you, hiding the gun in his pocket, and then he went toward the room-service room and I heard Sergio say that you had not come back for an order for a long time. I figured you must be with the old oilman."

"Whatever else, I've got to get the gun away from him."

"Oh, no! Why can't you just walk down to the terrace and around the front of the hotel and leave that way?"

But that is not what I decided—not that I think I was actually weighing choices—for I took Jean by the arm and we circled the hotel on the ocean side, coming back past the pool and entering the ground floor through a door in the latticework to reach Harry's office and, to our luck, Harry himself. He applied hydrogen peroxide to Jean's cut. Then he put a kettle on for tea, explaining she could calm herself with the brew and apply the wet leaves to the cut to keep it from leaving a scar. With my arm around Jean as she sat in one of Harry's scruffy chairs, I

129

stood admiring his deft hands, not saying a word.

"All right, kid. I know about it. Elmore phoned me fifteen minutes ago to say that George was going to shoot you. He said your ladylove here had taken his car. He was worried about the car. He's getting himself a lift."

"Where can I get Jean to go that's safe?"

"Right now, John, I think it's you that George is going to shoot. Put our mind to that."

There was no time. George pushed open the door to Harry's office and fell heavily against the jamb, because the door opened easily when he expected it to be barred. It was this forcing motion that gave Harry the chance, for the gun was in George's right hand, on the side that rebounded from the doorjamb, and he had to correct his position. I saw the gun clearly and was slowed by a bizarre wonderment. It was the same kind of pearl-handled, chrome-plated .38 Police Special that my godfather had left me as his sole legacy: a western show gun of sorts, ostentatious but deadly, a gun you would not prize in a collection but would not scorn as a weapon. I was staring into the dark hole of the barrel but I saw no flash when my arm jerked. As I fell backward I saw Harry's left hand hit George on the wrist with a wooden handle of some sort and, almost simultaneously, his right hand cuffed George's neck as he bent over.

Jean leaned over me, her breath on my mouth, and reached her hands under my shoulders as if to rock me, but quickly Harry pulled me up, straightened the chair, and lowered me into it. Together they took off my jacket and shirt and had got this far when Elmore and Sergio appeared together in the doorway.

"You killed my boy, you whoremaster!" Elmore shouted to me.

130

Harry looked at him disgustedly. "Elmore, use your eyes instead of your mouth. John here is shot. George is alive and breathing, even if I cold-cocked him to keep him from killing somebody with that Buffalo Bill gun."

Sergio took a handkerchief from his pants pocket and wiped his mouth. "I shall call the police," he said to Harry.

"No. No. You don't call the police," Jean cried loudly just as Harry was saying to me, "You're lucky after all, Big John," making my side burn with the tips of his big fingers, "because the bullet no more than nicked a rib. It laid a track through your arm, too, but you ain't shot through."

Sergio turned toward the doorway, saying, "I'll call an ambulance," but before he could take a second step into the workroom Jean reached him, seizing his arm fiercely.

"I'll get the hotel nurse to bandage him." She did not let go his arm. "There won't be any record of this, not with the police or the hospital. I mean it, Sergio. I don't want his name on records."

"Don't be excited! Okay! Okay!" Sergio pulled down the lapels of his tuxedo coat and shot his sleeves, offended by Jean's clutching. "I don't want any trouble. But you," he said to me, stepping to the doorway, "are fired."

Harry said, "Sergio, get the hell out of here." He left, squaring his shoulders, but Elmore had not moved and every half minute or so he would look down at his son, then at me, finally at Harry, repeating the cycle in precise order. While Jean went off to find the nurse, I held my sides, crouched as if I had a stomachache. Harry examined the back of George's neck, turned back his eyelids, and felt the carotid arteries with one hand at his throat as if to choke him. "This mean peckerwood is going to live, Elmore, but I don't want him ever coming into my office again." Together they lifted George and carried him outside.

When Harry came back later, he said that Elmore was driving George home because he came to inside the car and convinced Elmore that he didn't need treatment, just a shot of whiskey and a snooze. The six-gun stayed on the floor. When Jean returned, she picked it up and stowed it in Harry's desk drawer before the nurse arrived. I knew the nurse from serving her in the employees' dining room at the start of the summer. She cleansed my arm with alcohol, applied a powder, and bandaged it tightly.

"Were you shot?" she asked.

"No."

"That's good." Against my rib she placed a large plaster. "Probably you got too close to one of those fishing spears."

"That's right," I replied. "A lot of those are being thrown around these days." She patted me on the shoulder and left without saying anything to Jean. A few minutes later Harry came back, breathing hard and looking tired. He stood in the doorway and watched as Jean rested her hand lightly on my shoulder, posed as in an old-fashioned wedding photograph.

"Besides bleeding on my floor, John, what else have you got on your mind?"

"Well, Harry, it's a little hard to say. Last night I lost my money in a poker game. I got shot this morning, and was fired from my job ten minutes ago." I stood up, immediately feeling sick.

Harry left his office then and, half turned from us, said, "Sport, be sure to say good-bye." I was sure he did not expect to see me on his return.

It used to puzzle me—it still does—that the counselors of your youth assume you can identify and declare decisions like innings in your life. By the time I entered college I felt underprivileged in this respect alone. I never seemed to have to make choices, at least not the kind that were the subject of moralizing in Sunday supplements and YMCA pamphlets and *Liberty* articles. I knew people who actually went around talking about alternatives and the possible effects of taking certain actions. Preparing for college, they were urged by a parent or relative to consider "traveling first," or "taking advantage of a small campus." They could, presumably, talk about such decisions safely, the range of selection being too narrow to allow anything importunate.

My life didn't lend itself to such talk except once, when I was told by a high school teacher who had gone to Barnard that I ought to join the best fraternity at the university, it having invited me mostly to improve the club's academic average. "Do it, John. Otherwise, you won't know later that it was not really important." In any event, questions of choice, the expressions of one's possible position, were not for me a matter of class, not determined by my coming from an immigrant family and unschooled parents. Class distinctiveness did not seem, ultimately, to be applicable to me. I was already privileged by means of academic competition, already regarded as exceptional by a few people who made awards or wrote commendations, who could be disinterestedly generous. It was not class, but the charge of egotism, that troubled me. How does one speak individually yet respectably? How can one be original but not appear pretentious? How could I get the attention of persons who would not be able, firsthand, to place me by name or relation or residence? I did not really resent the fact that fools in comfortable company can command attention,

yet I fell into the confusion of ascribing some of my remarks to well-known figures, hoping to give my opinions
credibility. (Are those hundreds of epigrams under Anon-
ymous in Bartlett and Stevenson the bastards of people
like me who believed that criticism requires pedigree?)
Yet even for me there had to be real decisions, yes and no
choices, if I slowed my life long enough to see its drift.
Maybe now, for the first time, I was making a move that
could be described fatefully, and repeated years later
when someone would listen.

I was reflecting on all this, not irrelevantly though
somehow grotesquely, as I sat back to ease the pain after
standing. My side ached perversely, for my blood must
now be pumping more slowly than when I watched the
low comedy of George lying on the floor and Elmore
circling the actors with his wary eyes. Did Jean see that
I was struggling? She withdrew and looked out the dirty
window crisscrossed by the basement latticework, her
back to me and her wrists resting awkwardly on her hips.
She turned. "Does it hurt bad?"

"No. I'll live—this time anyway. Do you think George
will try again?"

"No." She paused. "No. None of it will be the same
again."

"What do you mean, Jean?"

"You'll go. I'll go. George will stay here."

"Where will you go? You can come with me."

"That can't help. I'm married to George, and if we went
away together he'd have the right to come after us."

"You can get a divorce. You can go to Reno." I stood up
and went over to her and kissed her cheek where the welt
was turning purple. I pressed my hand against one of her
breasts. Was it to reassure her that her body was unda-

134

maged and my desire unstinted? She reached around, put one arm on my good side, and kissed me on the lips with her mouth open, making me feel her own capacity.

"Johnny, listen to me. You haven't got any money. And you have to leave now. It takes time."

"We could go to Reno," I said. "Nita knows how it works."

She began to cry and put both her hands, clenched in supplication, to the sides of her head. I was undecided whether to touch her again. "I love you. I always will love you. But you can't do anything."

"I can, Jean. You know I can."

"We can't argue. I'm going to Pearl Harbor, where my dad is. He wrote me that I can work in the supply depot there. He's got a small house."

"Does he know you want to come?"

"I wrote him about you and me."

"Have you got enough money?"

Jean stepped back, making ready to leave. "I have money at home in a cedar jewelry chest, and I've got about three hundred dollars in the hotel credit union."

"But you can't go down the bay alone!"

"I won't. Do you think that Nita could go get my clothes and things if somebody drove her? Would she be afraid? Maybe Jackson could go with her."

That was how it turned out. The Greek let Jackson drive Nita down the spit in his Chrysler Imperial, a concession that Nita said Dolores forced upon him. Jean and I waited in Nita's room, where under the easing of pain I fell asleep almost at once. When Jackson and Nita returned with two suitcases and a laundry bag, Jackson insisted he take Jean to the San Diego station and stay with her until she caught the four-o'clock train to Los Angeles. Nita offered to go, but Jean said no. Jean ran three steps from the curb to where I stood on the sidewalk and swept her arms around my neck. I didn't hear anything she said. Did she ask a pledge or confess a fear? She ran to the car, and Jackson gunned the engine, pushing the accelerator as the clutch was half let out, making of their departure a getaway.

Nita came out of the shop as I stood looking down the boulevard. She circled me, a gamine, so that I would look down at her. Her dark head thrown back, she said to me gravely, rendering a prognosis, "You're going, I know. You don't need any more talk." She reached up to kiss my chin and tucked some bills into my shirt pocket. When I returned to the Greek's place I found that she'd given me four tens. Upstairs I put my clothes in a Navy duffel that Jackson had sold me, clear profit to him. I abandoned my books and on them left an envelope holding twenty dollars back rent. As I passed the storefront I could not tell whether my departure was noted. Certainly it was expected, for Jackson said that when he went to pick up the car at the Greek's he heard talk of the "Big Shoot-Out."

I walked away holding the duffel over the shoulder of my good side, feeling a little sick from the pain but perhaps also from the air, made viscous by the lowering clouds. It struck me as absurdly consoling to think that the weather, as in a Hardy novel, had been cosmically called up to suit the occasion. I reached the hotel before three o'clock and went to Harry's workroom, waiting a few minutes before it occurred to me to look at the spike on the desk, where there was this note: "Took my wife and kids to Dago. School starts tomorrow. Let me know where you will be. I don't write much. You will be O.K."

On Harry's desk I left a neat bundle: two pairs of white work pants, the red monkey jacket, the Ready Fix tie. I walked across the grass from the side of the hotel to the boulevard to wait for the streetcar.

Chapter

12

Pismo Beach I reached by way of the Cabrillo Highway, No. 1, hitchhiking on a furniture van out of Los Angeles. It was not a destination. It was the place where I stopped. The highway ran through the town between the hills and the ocean. I sat for more than two hours on the sidewalk curb, which here, as in Salinas and some other California coastal towns, was so high you could bend your knees and hunch over. At my back was a corner drugstore; across the road was the dim outline of the chalk cliff and, below, two meager streets that paralleled the highway. The air was warm and still. At first light I got up and walked the short block that ran down to the sea wall.

On the left was a building larger than the one-story ones opposite; on its street level was a movie house and over it a hotel of two floors. The marquee was braced by two cast-iron spears caught on loops screwed to the brickwork. The movie showing that week starred Charles Laughton, whose wife, Elsa Lanchester, was supposed to offer Shosh a job in that turnabout theater in L.A. Looking at the marquee sign, I remembered waiting in a movie house in Ogden, Utah, for the right time to return to the freight yards to hop a train west across the desert to Sacramento. One of the triple features that night in Ogden was an awkward, creaking movie with Charles Laughton and Lillian Bond, frankly called *The Old Dark House*. On the right-hand sidewalk I walked past a row of blue and pink plaster buildings, amusement-park style: a billiard parlor and The Pink Arcade and The Camelia Ballroom. Some had high-set windows with concave bottle-green panes like the cocktail bars built in my home city after Repeal.

I must have sat on the sea wall almost motionless for another two hours. Below, the sea was welling forward in combers like giant jellies. These split on the black rocks, showering and scouring. The ocean, like the desert, cleans itself.

Maybe because I was traveling from no direct impulse, proceeding observingly but not intently, I let my mind conceive just then that a man's character is picaresque. I thought of Philip in Somerset Maugham's novel. At times puzzled by common contrarieties, Philip kept looking for the pattern of his life, for the threads that underlay and could explain, if not justify, all our foreseen enmities and unworthy desires and wasteful conventions. But it was all too grand. Philip, I suddenly realized, simply did not know how to act. He was capable of being original, but he also wanted to be predictable, like the people who command the right demeanor in repeatable situations. Neither did I know how to act, or when on the moment to be satisfied. It was not for me awesome, not a profound ambition. I had no desire to name imperatives or to find first causes. I wanted to be able to think plain things: more, perhaps, to say plain things without the ornaments of pride. I wanted to confute intellectuals who expect simple people to be good out of rudiment, but will not indict themselves.

I wanted not to believe that "real" life contends with imagination by claims to events more intricately mean that the novelist dares. It was important to me that in the cheap hotel rooms above the theater at my back there must be no hidden crimes, no nasty stories worn from mouth to mouth. Even the Depression's bad times, which left some of the town's storefronts empty with black-painted windows, did not appear to be wrong. I was pervaded with the ache of realizing that my country was my place and to me it would never be threatening. I could leave this little cleared town or I could stay awhile, either, without its making a big difference to me later. I was simply not yet privy to the irony of my life. There may be no point, when you are alone, in regarding your life as exceptional.

From the furniture van several hours before, I had seen, lighted by a lamp on a high post, a sign on Route 166 intersecting Highway 1 that read SANTA MARIA 9 MILES. I got off at Pismo partly because in speculating whether to visit Elizabeth Petrie I did not want my judgment penalized by distance. Once I decided to go back south, I was soon picked up by a milk truck. The highway followed the Southern Pacific tracks and was lined on both sides by the huge twisted trunks of blue gum trees, from which hung long strips of gray-white bark. Because these very tall eucalyptus trees bound the side roads, too, they must have been planted long ago as windbreaks. This was not new California, not like some places down south; it remained farming and ranching country. After riding about fifteen miles, we crossed the bone-dry Santa Maria River. Near the bridge I saw a very small rodeo circle with a sign,

140

ELKS STOCK SHOW. Hawks planed overhead.

"Who are you?"

"I'm somebody Elizabeth knows," I told her mother as she stood inside the porch screen door.

"Is that all you are?"

"Listen," I said, quickly angered, "who else should I be?"

"I don't want you to be anything. I'm not sure that Elizabeth should see you."

"Then you know me."

"I've heard of you."

"It's a beginning then, Mrs. Petrie, isn't it? I just want to say hello to Elizabeth. Is she at Pomona already?"

"No, she's here. My husband died three weeks ago."

"I'm very sorry. I'm truly sorry."

"Elizabeth is at the store. It's on the main street across from the Isis Theater."

She was standing behind a cosmetics counter covered by jars of hand lotion, gold-colored compacts, Coty lipsticks stuck like cartridges in a cardboard display box. It was a neat drugstore with the pharmacy at the back, small soda fountain at the side, and racks of remedies opposite. She looked up and at once saw my duffel bag.

"John! Wonderful! Where are you going? Can you stay awhile?" She frowned in surmise.

"That may be up to your mother, Liz," I said, reaching across to kiss her lightly. "I've been by your house. She and I have already been at each other."

"Give her a break, John. She told you, I'm sure, my father just died. She's already worried about my leaving again."

"I'm sorry about your father. I don't blame her, Liz. I must look like a sailor who is over the hill."

"You're not, are you?" She smiled and leaned forward to put her fingers on my lips, a pretty blessing.

"No. I turned out to be a character in a melodrama. It's a long story." I saw in Elizabeth's excited smile a reprieve from my own doubt that I was in Santa Maria at all. I looked at her with a rising hopefulness. She was so open and engaging that her good looks were consistent.

"You can tell me it at home." She locked the store, kissing me twice on the sidewalks we took to her house, each time holding her arms loosely around my neck: it was an assured gesture, not urgent but intimate.

Elizabeth's mother said hardly a word as we ate lunch, nor did she object when Elizabeth offered me a bedroom, with dormer windows and wooden louvers, on the third floor. But before I dropped off to sleep that afternoon I heard her voice on the floor below: "I know he's intelligent, Betty. But that doesn't explain why he's here. You could just as well say he is Scandinavian or blind in one eye. It won't do. Why is he here?" She had a point. In a nice town like Santa Maria, a young man dressed in a blue work shirt and cotton pants carrying a duffel bag was, on the face of things, an intruder, troublesome but undefinable, not yet an invader who could or must be appeased.

The Petries put me up five days. I did not press my early biography on Mrs. Petrie, nor did she ask for it. Whether she became more tolerant of me I'm not even clear, probably because we remained unknown to each other. Now I can't recall exactly her appearance. Elizabeth eased her worry by telling her I was going to Los Angeles; and she did not object to our taking a ride out in the country to talk with a pharmacist in San Luis Obispo who had indicated he might be willing to come to work at Santa Maria.

We drove, coming back, through the hilly country where the arroyos run down from La Panza Range. When it was warm and dry, the hills looked like golden straw and the washes were dun. This was great countryside, well used but still open. I felt comforted by what I saw, fields ridged by lacy live oaks against the horizon and, farther down, huddled, the California buckeyes showing their late September leaves. Elizabeth was not in a hurry to return to the store. We did not stay long in San Luis Obispo. The pharmacist refused an offer of salary and insisted on a partnership were he to come to Santa Maria.

As we got to the little town of Conception, Elizabeth on a whim decided that we should stop and look for tamales. We found them at the Valencia Café on the main street, which lay uneventful in the noonday light. For no reason other than to prolong the day, we walked to the highway intersection, passing the Hop Tung Fong Benevolent Society and Yasanti's Hardware and La Simpatica Store. At the intersection it was obvious that zoning had not yet classified Conception. On one corner was a gas station; opposite was an incredible house of nineteenth-century Queen Anne style with bow windows obtruding as high as the third and fourth floors. At the roof corners the weather vanes were flying pennants of iron. The house, like the graveyard across from it, attested the town's age. On the fourth corner was a structure that Elizabeth, even in her home area, could not explain, a pagodalike stack of bins rising forty feet. Maybe it stored green produce cooled by water that dripped through the openings between gray weathered slat sides.

We entered the graveyard, which was dusty because the pathways and plots were laid with soft pebbles. Unexpectedly, some of the headstones were elaborately engraved with angels and with crosses twined with leaves of myrtle and laurel and olive. There were mausoleums no higher than three or four feet with tiny pillars and lintels and friezes. "They look pathetically like doghouses, don't they," Elizabeth said as we sat under a plane tree on the only bench in the cemetery. "It's not a place to reflect in."

"No," I replied, "but maybe one shouldn't rely on such places. Libraries are the worst place to read books."

"Will you go to Yale?" she asked suddenly. I had told her the day before in the drugstore—not when we were together on the island—that I had a one-year fellowship in graduate English study that I could take up as late as the fall term of 1942.

"I don't know. The best thing I do is school."

"But that's not fair!" Elizabeth protested. "What have you done other than wait tables?"

"Mix paint in a paint factory and carry sides of beef inside the cooler of a packing house."

"Those were summer jobs," she argued.

"Well, Liz, what does an English major do except teach? Which I don't want."

"I'm an English major, too, John," Liz said quietly, "but then, it's different for a girl. A girl like me is supposed to get married right after college." Her eyes glistened. She was right. A girl like her—her clean brushed hair turned under into a roll at her neck, her narrow waist defined by the standard college uniform of sweater and skirt, her even white teeth and her superb lilting legs—a girl like Elizabeth is the prize and captive of campus life, usually engaged by the beginning of her senior year. I could think of marrying Elizabeth right then.

"I don't know what to say," I replied.

"Of course you don't, John," she said. "We're not having a Soc. 201 discussion."

"Liz, I like you as much as any girl I've known. That's not romantic, is it?"

"No."

"I shouldn't have come. I'm off my stride. It's not to do with you. I guess I'm on the run, in a way."

"I know about it, John. My Pomona friend from the hotel, Marjorie, telephoned me yesterday."

"Jesus!"

"Did you love her?"

"Did?"

"I'm not going to say 'do.' I don't want you to love her."

"She's a nice girl, Liz. Whatever the crime is, I'm guilty."

"You could marry out of guilt! How awful!"

"How about gratitude?"

"That's as bad. I sound like a shrew. I don't know why men marry!"

"Out of boredom."

"And women out of curiosity."

"We read the same plays. We've got that," I said, putting my arm around her, and we kissed softly again, as we had done during the past few days sitting on the swing of her porch or as we paused walking downtown after supper to the Isis to see a movie.

"I intend that we should have a lot more, Johnny," and she kissed me again in the heat of the Conception graveyard. We rode back to Santa Maria in silence, the air thickening from the two-o'clock sun at our backs and the smudge of insects sent to their deaths against the bisected, prow-like windshield. I left Santa Maria for Los Angeles the next morning. Mrs. Petrie stayed home until I left so that Elizabeth and I were not left to accident alone in the house. She even offered to drive me to the bus station, but I refused so that we could avoid awkward gestures of good-bye on the street.

The express bus stopped at Santa Monica. From there I took a local bus eastward along Sunset Boulevard to the 8200 block. At what I took to be the start of "The Strip," a name pronounced familiarly by the waiters at the hotel when commenting on the high life of Hollywood, I found, rising high above a little peninsula of property next to the Strip, the Chateau Marmont, a Mont-Saint-Michel of a hotel and apartment house with Gothic vaults, pointed windows, a stone fountain inside the main entrance, and at the rear, fire escapes fashioned in Romanesque black-metal trefoils. On the street behind, running between the Marmont and a steep hill, I found the house, its garage and gate of white metal and wood blocking from the street view a beautiful hanging garden full of pepper trees and yellow acacia and the lavender blooms of jaca-randa.

"I didn't think you would come," Arthur's mother said to me once I'd been admitted to the house by a maid.

"I didn't either. I have to ask you, what do I call you? You put your married name on the address you gave me, but the maid just said 'Miss Dawson.'"

"Don't, please, age me unnaturally. Call me Lelia. And are you still 'Big John'?"

I smiled down at her, suddenly realizing that I was still carrying the duffel bag over my shoulder as if I had just stepped off a liberty boat. "Probably not. I've been cut down in size since I saw you. 'John' will do."

"You are not going to graduate school, I take it. It is past that sort of time, isn't it?"

"No, I'm not. Is the job tutoring Arthur open? Maybe since he's started school in Brentwood, he doesn't need it."

"It is nice of you to remember where he goes to school. He's there but I also would like him tutored."

"You know that I am not a teacher?"

"Whatever you tell Arthur will occupy him and probably delight him. I am not clever in this respect. I don't know much about curriculums."

"It may be not much more than talking to him."

"If you will answer his questions, it will help greatly. It is what a child needs most from an adult. Arthur's father is gone, as you know, and I'm making movies—in fact, I won't be here for the next three weeks. I'm on location in the Tetons."

"Are you playing the rich and spoiled English owner of a ranch?"

"However did you know?" She laughed beautifully, as I remembered her doing at the hotel, by bringing her hands to a point under her chin and throwing her head back. "I must show you your digs."

A hard-packed clay path made hairpin turns after passing doors to the second and third floors of the house, and it rose to the top of the hill to stop at the fenced-off street that ran above the whole property. Every step of the way was planted with low bushes and flowers. Jacaranda and cockspur corals were seated neatly in saucers of recently watered loam. My "digs" were a room and bath in a one-story cottage at the top of the path. The gardener, who had the two remaining rooms, always used a gate to the street above, while I used the main street entrance. It was a small distinction but one suitably English, as if I were a county family's clergyman.

In the small dining room off the kitchen, I ate breakfast and dinner with Arthur, lunch on my own while he was at school, but when Lelia returned from location there were times when I joined guests in the dining room of the house. Sometimes she came in to eat with me in the kitchen if she was kept late at the studio. On those occasions I picked at my second dinner plate out of obligation. Arthur was, as his mother predicted, occupied by my presence. He dogged me everywhere, running up the path, puffing and rubbing his thighs rough red, to see me in the cottage when he got home from his private school. He would jump on my bed to catch his breath and begin every conversation with a bit of impressive information. "Do you know, Big John, that the Chinese paint gods over their doorways. To protect them. Like god doorkeepers." I soon learned to make connections with these rhetorical questions and would either look up things in the *Encyclopaedia Britannica* in the main house or go to the library on North Ivar Street. Arthur and I painted the kitchen god, Tsao-shen, and pasted him above the big electric range, to the cook's displeasure. We made two versions of Kuan-kong at his urgent suggestion once he learned that this figure could be the god of literature and valor, or, alternately, the god of peace and war. Arthur insisted I keep Kuan-kong in the cottage in his first incarnation, while he posted him as warrior over his own bed on the third floor.

Having never before traveled as an adult, letter writing was something in which I had little practice. I did write my father twice from the island to tell him I was safe.

Now, in the cottage above Lelia's house, I wrote two letters at one sitting, one to Harry telling him my address and asking him to let me know if he found out Jean's address, and the other to Nita at the print shop—though I later found out the letter reached her at Las Vegas—to ask after her and to repeat the request about Jean. I heard from neither, nor from Jean. Of course, it was possible to write to her father. His first name was unknown to me, but I knew his rank and his duty at Pearl Harbor. But a minatory unease prevented me. I thought about Jean almost every day, and at night I dreamed of our being together, yet at moments I mistrusted my feelings. I could, I knew, become a stranger to my own past.

Arthur was not keen to take exercise despite Lelia's urging us. About all I managed was to take him walking along the streets of downtown Hollywood, and even this was not in aid, because we ended up buying Eskimo Pies or perching on stools to drink root beer at a drive-in constructed like a keg. We sat one afternoon, I think the third day I arrived, and as the mugs were set down, we pledged never to drink more than one apiece of the ten-cent Giant size (presumably twice the volume of the Large mug). Arthur drank his Giant without once putting it down on the counter. He kept squirming in an attempt, imitating me, to hook his toes to the back rung of the stool. If he was interested in why I was in Hollywood, which on his request I fell to explaining, he was too bright and too courteous to believe that I was present entirely because of him.

"Didn't your father want you to come home, Big John?"

"He knew I would go somewhere else."

"But you could have gone anywhere. That's right, isn't it, Big John? Like a hobo catching a freight?"

"Sure. I came here, maybe, because of the movies."

"I guess you like stories. I do, too."

Arthur asked for another drink, arguing that a new rule ought not be enforced retroactively, that we had made the restriction only after sitting down. I laughed and agreed. We blew the foam from the mugs and it fell like spittle to the sidewalks, drying into spots.

"John, it's the stories you like, isn't it?" he repeated, because I had not replied.

"Yes, Arthur, the stories. They begin and end without doubt. It's like going to school and having the teacher give you all the answers and then call recess."

"Big John, you went to school like me! It's not like that."

"Well, I guess so. Maybe Hollywood is the same as everywhere else."

Arthur looked startled and touched my knee—he'd never touched me before, except in games or roughhousing in his room.

"I'm not leaving, Arthur. One thing, I'd like to write a movie story."

"What kind of story?"

"Something simple. Something without doubt." I feigned a punch at his crab-apple cheeks as he wiped the last drops of the root beer from his mouth. When he made prefatory remarks leading to another drink, I picked him off the stool. "Damn it, Arthur, you're turning into a drunk. I'm taking you home to sober up before supper."

In his room Arthur kept small barbells and when Lelia suggested that he might use them better in my room, I had to carry them up the path. But going downtown was some exercise, several miles of walking, and it served to give new subjects for our discourse—to examine and immediately discard out of uninterest or ignorance, or to pursue until Arthur's or my energy flagged, usually mine.

150

We would walk past the movie houses, the Pacific's marble front and fretted iron lamps, the Alhambra's fan palms
guarding Moorish doorways, and Arthur's favorite, the
Pantages with its King Tut figures. Around the corner
from the Pantages he found a tattoo parlor and each time
his eyes were fixed by the specimens displayed as photo-
graphs in the street window. We could not see into the
dim interior, but Arthur never tired of inspecting the
especially exotic work: a woman's back with three eyes
peering from the foliage and scrollwork, a sailor's breasts
made into rose windows with "1926" over one nipple and,
over the other, "USA." On Saturdays, oddly, we never
went to the movies. Arthur did not want to sit still without
talking. Perhaps he was already blasé, listening to his
mother's casual mention and introduction of other movie
stars. He had met Kay Francis, Clive Brook, Jack Holt, and
Madeleine Carroll, he told me as a matter of fact.

Sometimes the chauffeur, a dour middle-aged man
whose accent I could not really place but assumed was
Balt, was commandeered on Arthur's pleading so that we
could ride to Griffith Park, rising eastward under the
proclamation HOLLYWOODLAND stuck on the Hollywood
Hills with rather unsubstantial white cutout letters. We'd
never fail to take notice of the castle on Franklin Street,
which Arthur and I decided was the prison holding the
Man in the Iron Mask. Passing the Montecito Hotel, he
would let me know that he was attentive to everything I
commented on by saying that it was like the Marmont,
"early Gothic." I'd reply, "Better early than late," and he
would giggle at the exchange of esoteric remarks. At
Griffith Park we visited the Planetarium and then sat on
the seats before the deserted open stage of the Greek
Theater, eating popcorn. Above, in the October light, the

Hollywood Hills were browned except for the oases where houses hung.

On those trips we went sometimes to Hollywood High, which I did not expect to be so new. I had imagined it as the font of stardom as early as the days of *The Squaw Man.* Arthur and I sat watching football practice or took our baseball gloves and tossed a ball, which we could not do at home because the paths were steep and a missed ball was usually a lost ball. One day Arthur looked at the inscription around the Liberal and Household Arts Building, *Equality Breeds No War,* and asked me what it meant. I told him rather sternly that it did not make any difference what it meant, for it was not true. He kept asking me why it was not true and reminded me that I had told him, in describing my riding the rails, that everybody on the road was the same and that was why they got on so well together. I told him some things were true in particular but not in general. Arthur was hurt when the talk turned tough—and mysterious.

Chapter

13

"What do you teach him?" Lelia asked after a period during which I saw little of her except at sporadic after-work late meals when Arthur was long asleep.

"I don't know that I'm teaching him anything. He excavates me like a quarry: I may run out."

"What will you do then?"

"Well, I won't turn to the unknown. I don't handle religion." Lelia nodded in amusement and I went on: "Anyway, the only thing sacred to Arthur and me is baseball statistics."

"I'm relieved! I can tell that Arthur's only care is that you will leave."

"Not yet. Of course, sooner or later, everything must happen."

"You told me this summer that you were trying not to have a future. I thought it a most admirable ambition."

"Funny thing, Lelia. It's impossible not to have a future unless you are a hobo."

Stories about my brief experience riding the rails, along with less exotic Americana, were what I related to Arthur just before he turned in. We'd sit opposite, Arthur drawing up his feet in imitation but not quite being able to clasp his knees, on the deep window seat of his bedroom. It was paneled on the sides and held a maroon cushion. He wanted always to darken the room so that we could see beads of light on Sunset. Lelia said that we looked like Maxfield Parrish figures out of one of Arthur's books. Arthur's large round head was fitted by curly hair that wound more tightly after his evening bath, and I wore a sailor's cap I had brought from the island. In the gloom of Arthur's room we may indeed have played Parrish's minstrels and fools in their felt crowns.

Arthur understood that hoboing is special because the hobo is on the road without destination, the journeying its own purpose. "If you are a hobo, Art—and of course there are boy hobos—what happens is you go without going anywhere. If you stop, it's only to move on again." I could not convey to him how touched I was—during my week or so with those freight riders—by the unpronounced effect of the hobo's life. It is a palinode, a retraction against all the rest of us, who believe that there is a place for everyone and don't know that you can be recruited only if you are found.

"Are hobos ever mean, Big John?"

"They are chased by the bulls, but they don't fight back."

"The bulls are railroad policemen, right?"

"Right. No, Art, hobos are not mean."

"You told me your mother said they were a pack of wild dogs."

"She didn't mean it. She always gave them food at the back door when we lived close to the Burlington tracks. Anyway, hobos can't be a pack. They don't organize. They're friends but they don't order each other around."

"Like you and me, Big John."

"That's right. Hobos always ask about each other. They say, 'Have you seen Modesto Whitey?' or 'I last saw Little Omaha Red in St. Louis.'"

"Why can't we have names like that?"

"We can. Who do you want to be?"

Arthur put one hand over his mouth in glee and said, "I'll be 'Little John.'"

"I tell you what. You be 'Gila Junction Art.' And I'll be 'Carson City John.' How's that?"

"Will we live in a jungle like hobos?"

"Not right away. You know, Gila Junction, hobos are smart. In big towns or switching yards, they set up jungles at both ends, one for hobos going north, the other for hobos going south."

"And they cook stew in tin cans and chew tobacco."

"Gila Junction, it's the time to put your head down on your bindle and go to sleep."

"I know what a bindle is. It's like a Boy Scout pack."

"Listen, go to bed. And stop dropping your pajama pants or else Miss Starrett will get us."

"Big John, you know Miss Starrett is gone! You know that!"

"Yeah, but how do we know she's not watching us from somewhere?"

Arthur shivered and pulled at his waistband and fell into bed.

It was Lelia who heard the story of how I reached California, the parts that were not suitable for Arthur's ears. She came back late one night from Warner Brothers, where she was "lent out" by RKO, which held her contract. We sat at a white table covered by Formica (which I'd never seen before coming to California). Lelia ate hungrily from a casserole the cook had left to warm, and I smoked steadily after chewing down a few bits of chicken. She said I was obsessively exaggerating the independence of the drifter's life, although she did not mind Arthur's fascination, which she took to be a passing form of male bravado like admiring cowboys and pirates.

"Not for me, Lelia. I think hobos ought to be preserved. Because of good times, there are fewer and fewer. But of course to cherish a hobo is to deny him."

"Cherish! It sounds decadent."

"Only politically," I said. "The hobo is the last anarchist left in America. The Wobblies are gone and the fight was lost in Barcelona."

"It all seems so long ago, all of it." And it did, I thought, yet it remained unsettled like so much of the past. Had Bakunin ever heard of hobos? Would he think it possible to be anarchist but neither rebellious nor radical?

Lelia guessed at the subject of my silence. "Are you interested in politics, John?"

"No. Just war, maybe."

"But between liberals and conservatives? You must be a liberal."

"I'm not sure. In California, I've noticed, conservatism is the privilege of the many, not the few." It did not seem illogical to me. The hobos I met did not want to expose society or get even with it, which more or less amounts to the same thing. They probably would accept that governments are reformed by leaders, not by followers, which conservatives believe as well.

Lelia said, "If someone has no political interest, as I confess I don't, then one ought to settle for being as kind as possible. I don't know whether that's being liberal or conservative. Probably Saint Francis said it."

"Ben Franklin."

"You are impossibly American!" Lelia cried. "Tell me how you really got to California: did you ride the rails all the way?"

"I did a good part of the way when I ran out of hitchhiking, which was in Cheyenne, where I caught a freight and sat in an open cattle car just as it was pulling out for Utah. For some reason—the freight was made up in Cheyenne, only a hundred and fifty miles away—it stopped in Rawlins. I walked to the western edge of Rawlins to thumb a ride and got as far as Rock Springs before I was stuck. On the far end of that town there was no car traffic and so I went into a bar to cool off with a beer. Two blond girls were in there, good-looking and well dressed. They began to tell me of their plans to go to South America on tour as actresses. I decided to be convinced. It seemed rather pointless not to be. Pretty soon a huge guy, six and a half feet, with hands like hammers, came in. He was wearing a white Stetson and had parked outside a white convertible—the best car I've ever seen, an old Marmon, four doors on a straight line from the wings on the radiator. The girls told him I was a new friend and that I wanted a ride across the Wasatch range into Utah. I still don't know how far they themselves were going that way. I couldn't figure out which one was his girl, because he hugged and kissed them alike and called each of them Dolly. But I found out soon enough. He got in front with one after the other insisted she'd ride in back with me. We had gone about ten miles at a fast clip when she edged up next to me and all of a sudden swung her legs across my lap. He slammed on the brakes, skewing that great car across the concrete highway. I climbed right over the back, probably kicking a hole in the folded canvas top, ran down the highway as fast as I could go, though I was woozy from the beer and the heat. He chased me a hundred feet or more, then settled for cussing. I could hear the two Dollys yelling in unison, 'Go, go, go,' whether urging the cowboy or me I never found out.

"I stopped for four nights in a hobo jungle on the western edge of Green River, until I found a freight that took me through Fort Bridger to Ogden, where I again stayed with hobos because the yards were full of railroad cops. A switchmaster saw me hanging around and told me to come back at eleven at night, when a UP freight was going out. He said that he'd leave the seal open on the third to last car so I could get in. He didn't want any money and he didn't trick me. When I came back I found the car unsealed, slid back the door, and climbed in. A guy grunted as I nudged him getting in. I struck a light. He was young like me and dressed about the same, and he yelled to me to put out the match, else 'we'll get our heads beat.'

"The next morning, when the train stopped in Winnemucca, Nevada, we found out the boxcar was swept clean except for in front of the doors, where we had slept. This guy was from Colorado College, going to Seattle to stay with his brother. When the train stopped in Winnemucca we fell to arguing over the comparative merits of big league hitters and forgot that when freight cars move backward and forward several times they are probably being shunted to a sidetrack.

"We spent the day waiting in Winnemucca, which looks like a western movie set fronting the UP tracks, and had to settle for an oiler coupled right behind the engine. We came roaring down through hillside cuts holding on to the iron handrail at the side of the oiler. Hot coals and flakes

158

of ash flew backward into our ears and eyes. When we saw the sign for Sparks, the switching yard just outside Reno, we knew we had to jump, because back in Winnemucca at the water tower an old hobo had told us that the Sparks bulls were extra mean. 'They use billies before they jail you,' he said. We were not smart in choosing our spot when we went sailing off, pumping our legs to hit the steep bank on the run. We tore our hands and faces as we lost the pace and went rolling to the bottom on cinders and shale chips.

"We walked into Reno and I stopped a police car to ask where we could sleep for a buck. The policeman pointed out a place and said, 'If you guys are going to be vagrants, you got to stop asking for directions.' I parted with the Colorado College guy in Reno. I have no idea whether he got to Seattle; he took to Reno like a drunk to drink. I found a freight headed for Sacramento and this time shared a car with a Negro who explained his wearing seven shirts: it saved wrapping a bindle. There was also an old guy who had a small sick dog and kept looking at it mournfully. The dog seemed to appreciate it. Neither the Negro nor the old man talked until I told them where I was going. The Negro was headed for Eureka and the old man said he'd 'lay over' in Sacramento until the dog got well. They agreed I'd have to ride the rods out of Sacramento. The Negro said it was 'all sealed freight' into Oakland.

"And that's what I did, though first I needed instructions from a hobo in Sacramento who had an honest face like Jack Holt. It was pretty awful under the car, next to the wheels, what with the risk of letting go your feet or your hands. It's like fighting sleep. You are lulled by the ties running by so fast that they seem to pile up, while the

159

wheels at your head go 'it-tick-it-tick' on and on, and after a while you get used to it and that's when it gets dangerous."

"That's all?" Lelia asked. I laughed. "I cannot understand why you wanted to do it. What did you hope to find?"

"Nothing much," I said.

"Do you like California that much?"

"I wonder at it."

"Well, it's time that you wondered some more. Come to the party I'm giving on Saturday. It will be your first."

That was how I met Zernbach, at Lelia's party, and Winterfield, too, and how I came to be paid to write parts of scripts that probably were not made into movies. A Hollywood party's magic shines for the outsider like a kaleidoscope: the actual incidents (if they can be known) and the fanciful accounts in print are thrown together like shards of colored glass and made to change into whole designs by the twin mirrors of the viewer's envy and desire. Everyone seems to hope that if the Hollywood scene is not elegant, then it will be notorious. Even now I have no information that is useful, for I went to only two of Lelia's parties and once to Winterfield's above Malibu. I heard of grand gatherings at Santa Monica Beach, where Darryl F. Zanuck lived and where William Randolph Hearst built a compound for Marion Davies. There was a permanent rumor that in the "Colony" at Malibu there were hideaways where privacy ensured by affluence allowed all kinds of depravity. Winterfield told me he ascribed the persistence of such gossip to the fact that Malibu was cut off initially from Santa Monica on the coast road and still seemed remote to a society that thrived on publicity but sought ways to avoid it momentarily.

Winterfield repeated the story of Frederick Hastings Rindge, a Harvard man who bought the old Spanish-grant Rancho Malibu and built a country estate there. He lived in Santa Monica, a devout businessman and busy churchman who wanted Malibu kept uninhabited, not only the beach but also the headlands above Coral and Topanga canyons, and between them Malibu Canyon, where Winterfield's own house was. "There is no persuasion so dedicated as that of a convert who is also a widow," Winterfield said. "When Rindge died in 1905, his wife kept a promise to him to fight off any development of Malibu. She did it for more than twenty years. You see, the Southern Pacific coastal line ran north up to Santa Monica, and south down from Santa Barbara, but between them was this missing link, the most desirable stretch of coastline in the world probably. To satisfy the state laws, Rindge built a railroad of his own to keep the SP out. It was a rickety twenty-mile narrow-gauge line called 'Hueneme, Malibu and Port Los Angeles Railroad.' He died right after it was built and Rhoda May Rindge—I once knew her well—took up the fight against the SP, the oil companies, the whole California real estate lobby. She hired gunmen on horses to ride the Rancho Malibu. Imagine it! Make-believe westerns were being filmed in Santa Monica Canyon when a few miles away the last range war in America was being fought for real. She lost in the end, of course, and the SP laid its tracks, and thirteen years ago the highway was finished, the one you came down this summer to reach Los Angeles. Even so, she owned most of the Malibu property on which the actors and producers rented houses. In the leases she put a prohibition against drinking, true Rindge to the last, as if United States law was not to be trusted, which in the case of the Volstead Act it was not. Nobody down there on the beach," he said, gesturing toward the edge of the palisade, "can recall anything of this, not even between drinks and copulations, but then, most movie people think Southern California was sprung full blown from the head of Adolph Zukor or, at the least, Leo Carillo."

Winterfield did not tell me this at my first party at Lelia's—I met him later—but at that party I did meet Zernbach. In Lelia's house, the living room or sitting room (neither term seems to suit) was two stories high with a gallery running around three sides beginning and ending at the wall where high arched windows looked onto the front garden. The gallery connected bedrooms on the second floor, but there was space at one end for musicians, on this occasion a pianist and two violinists and two horn players. Music made Lelia's dinner parties memorable, everybody said. What was played I do not recall and in any event could not hear too well. There were loud greetings and farewells as entrances and departures were made irregularly, and the murmur of talk was broken with cries of dismay or disbelief over some piece of news and barks of laughter, mostly from the women.

I did not go down to be seated at dinner, on the excuse I wanted to stay with Arthur. My delay was in fact caused by my not having a suit, but when I did come down in slacks and a jacket I was not really discomfited. I suppose that Lelia made it appear that as a resident I traversed the house at my leisure. She introduced me as "my son Arthur's tutor, John Sirovich," and stayed until she found for me a knot of guests she must have felt assured would talk agreeably. This turned out to include a woman costume designer at Paramount who was short and smoked incessantly through a short cigaret holder that looked like pure onyx, and her escort, a silver-haired man who told me he was a lawyer for Paramount, and a producer called "Marty," who didn't say anything at first but looked at me from time to time from behind the heaviest pair of horn-rimmed glasses I'd seen. The costume designer asked if I was trying to get into the movies, and when I said no, she said she didn't believe it. "You already are in," the lawyer said in taking up the case. "Being seen by movie people makes it real."

"Like trees falling in the forest that don't make a sound unless someone is listening?"

"Please don't say anything profound," Lelia told me, moving off. "You'll frighten the guests."

"Who the hell are you?" the producer with the goggled glasses asked me.

"I'm tutoring Miss Dawson's son."

"What, he don't go to school?"

"He does. I spend time with him after school."

"What in hell for?" I didn't reply. "What about Lelia?" His tone had not changed; it was evenly insistent. I looked at him closely. He was drinking, as was everyone else, but it was still early and he didn't look drunk.

"And? And? What else do you do after school?"

The lawyer moved away then, and this somehow signaled. The volume of talk around our group slowly subsided. People were listening, I realized. "And? And? You guys used to be called tennis coaches."

That is when I did it. I reached over and withdrew his glasses from his head, like pulling out an electric plug, and with the other hand I took his glass and put it down on the floor. He was blinking, his pupils widening, when I straightened up and jammed my left forearm across his belly. There was no noise as he fell in place, as if he'd been

163

standing in a crowd. I did not step away when the designer screamed. "Brutal!" She pointed up at me with her cigaret holder. "He's a Nazi!" Lelia arrived, looking concerned, but said nothing while two men puffed away at lifting the unconscious Marty, allowing him to sag in the middle. Then, a series of suggestions was offered. Someone urged that he be carried to the kitchen, for reasons that were obscure; another accused the people who had not risen from a nearby settee of being callous; finally the two bearers, tired and undecided, put Marty back on the floor, where his pulse was taken and his eyelids rolled back by a tall man. He pronounced Marty alive and probably unhurt and encouraged four men, this time, to carry him to a car on the street, saying he would make a call to the nearby clinic in Beverly Hills. While this proceeded I heard versions of what had happened: I was a gatecrasher to the party who had been properly challenged by Marty; I was a hired bouncer from Ciro's, on the Strip, who thought poor Marty to be offensively drunk. Lelia moved away and signaled to the piano player on the gallery to start up.

"Tell me something, kid, but only if you are not insanely offended by questions from innocent bystanders," I heard a hoarse voice behind me. "Just what did old Marty say that got him a no doubt deserved punch in the gut."

"No, I don't mind," I told the short and roundly muscled man who stood flicking the ash of a cigar into an empty highball glass. His brown eyes were wry, I thought, but then made a strange note to myself that expressions can be wry but organs cannot. I was self-conscious. "I don't know who he is. We didn't talk. He wanted to know what I did for Lelia besides tutoring her son."

"He's a schmuck. But why did you hit him? Whose

honor were you defending? No need to answer that."

"Why not?"

"When a guy hits another guy, a man's honor is at stake."

"My father, who believes in feuds, would agree with you."

"You carried me too far there."

"Who was the doctor who looked at Marty?"

"That Doctor Kildare is not a doctor, John—it is John, right? He was once, years ago, your employer's boyfriend. He owns some oil wells down at Wilmington."

"Oh."

"My name is Jules Zernbach."

"I'm John Sirovich."

"What are you doing in Hollywood?"

"I came here to work because I was broke. I guess, too, I'm looking around. I've got a graduate fellowship to Yale in literature that I've not yet decided to use."

"Do you write?"

"I don't know. I've published two stories and a few poems. I once wrote a five-act closet drama."

"That's the way to write movie scripts."

"Are you a scriptwriter?"

"I am a hell of a lot more nervous than that, John O'Sullivan. I commission writers and buy scripts at RKO. I'm a vice president, which means I have no excuses."

"Only artists have excuses?" I suggested.

"They need them. It is a hell of a thing to be serious on schedule."

"Shakespeare was," I replied.

"Yeah, there's always Shakespeare, but then, he had a percentage."

I laughed for the first time that evening, and Zernbach

looked up and punched my shoulder and said, "Listen, come round. I live on North Rodeo in Beverly Hills."

I moved then to go outside. Lelia watched my leaving as she stood near one of the big windows holding a glass I knew to be soda water, for she did not drink. I hesitated, to give her a chance to talk to me, but she shook her head slightly. I went out and walked up the path past the second-floor door, out of which lapped the renewed conversation of the party, past the third floor, where Arthur was snoring, and up the garden to the cottage. I sat down heavily on the bed and for a time considered that I might go down to the Strip and look around. By the time that thought was sent back and forth between the positive and negative charges in my mind, I felt drowsy. Soon I was asleep, fully clothed, to the sound of music rising.

Chapter

14

Movie people always complain they do not see enough of each other and ought more often to get together. For stars and directors and producers—but not studio heads, from whose peerage no one is absent—it is a test of popularity that makes them call across restaurant tables and cabanas and even from passing automobiles on Wilshire with cries of recognition followed by accusations that they were not together the night before or the week previous. Winterfield told me, when I visited him at the ranch above Malibu Beach, that the publicized back-and-forth life of Hollywood Hills, Beverly Hills, Bel Air, Brentwood, and Pacific Palisades was ordinary except for the unmistakable presence of hierarchy.

The butler left me on the doorstep to check whether Mr. Zernbach was at home or not. Bands of chrome ran across the second-story windows at the corners. A stack of glass brick rose from the front door to the flat roof. The front door opened onto a tiled courtyard that ran to the white iron gate at the street. In the middle was a two-tiered fountain like a cake stand. Such chaste "moderne" houses were found next to luxurious California mission-style houses and others that seemed to have been moved from studio sets. Opposite Zernbach's house was a huge imitation of the Alhambra that reminded me of a theater at home with three portals framed by colored tiles in reverse curves, the center to buy your tickets, the right to go in, and the left to go out.

Zernbach was not surprised that I had so soon taken up his invitation, but mentioned it in his own way. "I take it," he said when I emerged from the back of the house into a colonnaded cloister next to a swimming pool, "that you just happened to be walking up North Rodeo and saw me fanning myself on the front porch."

"Something like that. But I haven't seen a front porch in Beverly Hills."

"Listen, the only front porches around here are on sets. In movies, front porches are Booth Tarkington. Nobody plans robberies or falls dead on them. Jimmy Cagney had to fall dead through the front door right into his sainted mother's living room."

"Who decides things like that?" I asked, seating myself without invitation in a white iron chair opposite the chaise longue on which Zernbach lay wearing swimming trunks.

"Who decides?"

"Well, are the sets described in detail in the scripts," I asked by way of reminding him of my mission.

"Oh, that. How things look is the director's job and the producer's choice. The screenwriter writes a plot and dialog that will be rewritten by another writer and another and so on. Only the rewriting is hard. The original ends up as one paragraph told in a story conference: See, there's this white kid who was captured by Indians when he was only six; when the sergeant at the fort rescues him, he wants to go back being an Indian, only in the end he leads the soldiers to the Indians, who are holding his sister a hostage—I hope you get the horror; we all know how horny Indians are—and the soldiers wipe out the savages; the kid himself, taking the pistol from his dying buddy sergeant, shoots the chief, who you can tell is the chief because the camera cuts to him three or four times looking constipated on his horse."

"I seen it," I said. "A swell movie."

Zernbach said, "Don't get the idea writing a script is hard. Getting the right story and casting, that's hard."

"What sells, then? What subject?"

"Somebody said once there are only four basic plots in the world; every other is a variation. Who said that?"

"Aristotle, probably."

"I give it to him."

"Which four?"

"You see more movies than I do," he challenged.

"Sex. Fighting. Money. Politics."

"Not bad. I wouldn't back a movie that was mostly politics—well, not unless the politicians are wearing robes and torturing Christians." Zernbach leaned over, folds of skin forming. "Pictures about politics are a hard sell. And blind people. And Eskimos."

"But what about Frank Capra?"

"He makes politics a big American family. It's just that bad uncles like Edward Arnold and Claude Rains screw up. Then they're sorry. Their rimless glasses mist over at the end."

"Movies can't elect, I suppose."

"Tell me, if you wanted to start a revolution and had a million dollars, would you make a picture with it?"

"No. But if the revolution was won, I might spend a

million explaining how glorious it was."

"Would you tell the truth?" Zernbach asked.

"I wouldn't know it."

"Right. I tell you—and it is not Aristotle but me telling you—that propaganda needs only a little truth; it needs a lot of drama. I always figure that Hitler is hard put to use much recent history. He can't praise the Kaiser, who was a loser; and Bismarck never was a hero to the Bavarians and Austrians. Hitler uses a little Wagner and a lot of Hollywood to stage spectaculars in Nuremberg. It strikes me that the new Eisenstein movie, *Nevsky,* is not much different from the Hitler news pictures except for the director. German photography is better. Still, the Soviets love film. Merian C. Cooper was an aviator in the last war and somehow ended up in a Russian camp. He met Albert Boni, the publisher, there and Boni told him that he had come to Russia to sign up authors. An official introduced Boni to Lenin just as a cameraman asked Lenin to walk toward him; not to waste time, Lenin took Boni by the arm and started to walk forward, talking to him. Let's face it, waiting as long as he did to become a star, Lenin was not going to blow a take. For twenty years now, every Soviet movie opens, not with the national anthem, but with Lenin walking side by side with Albert Boni, not understanding a word of Russian or German."

I said, "Lenin probably was saying, 'What's more, Trotsky doesn't even look Russian.' "

Zernbach laughed in short huffs. "Or else, 'I advise against the meat loaf at the Majestic.' "

"I couldn't write on politics," I said.

"You think it's dirty?"

"No. I don't despise it."

"That's good. There is nothing wrong with politics except that it's necessary."

"I have decided," I told Zernbach, "not to be cynical about anything unless I want to reform it."

"I'll steal that line from you, John, if I can find somebody who will understand it. It's a problem, believe me. Nobody has any politics out here. It's like religion. If you get serious about it, you might hurt somebody's feelings —maybe your own. The dumb things people say in this town. There's a thing going around now. You meet a Catholic and to make him feel better you say, 'Oh, you're a Catholic. I wish I were.'" Zernbach leaned back and laughed. "Of course, it won't work with Jews. The line has to be changed: 'Oh, I'm a Jew. I wish you weren't.'" Zernbach quickly dived into the pool, the water spurting onto my shoes. He swam compactly, light glistening off the tight curls of hair on his shoulders. As I watched I felt the social disadvantage of waiting on another who is doing something that should be mutual, like sitting in a parlor while in the next room somebody eats his dinner. Zernbach pulled himself out of the pool in a single strong motion and walked toward me shaking his legs and arms like a bear. He cocked one ear, then the other, picked up a terry-cloth robe, and walked into the house.

I followed him, uninstructed and irritated. I will never make a good guest, I told myself, recalling the occasion when I was invited to luncheon by the dean of the law school at the university during spring recess. He took me to his club in our home city, a blocky building of red sandstone with granite keystones. I felt immediately the victim of ritual, of secret propriety. After climbing the main staircase inside, at the top I had to pause because I had been signaled to go ahead of him without knowing whether to turn left or right. It happened again at the door of a huge paneled dining hall because he again politely had let me lead the way onto strange ground. As the captain approached, the dean asked me whether I wanted to face the windows or the center of the room. The question was so precious that my nervousness disappeared on the moment. "The windows," I said with authority.

Inside the house, in what looked like a fraternity house game room, I recognized a Barcelona chair. I'd seen one only in illustrations. Zernbach asked the Filipino houseboy to bring us fruit juice. "Politics," he said reflectively, as if reintroducing the subject to himself. "Let me tell you it's practiced here by real jewel cutters."

"It's New York, isn't it, that has the real power in the movies?" I asked.

"Why do you say that?"

"The other night you said New York was stopping one picture and holding up another so that two stars could work on a third picture."

"So?"

I didn't reply. "But you admit," Zernbach said, "that it's me you are asking about some work, not New York."

"Yes. I didn't mean it that way. You start things, obviously."

"Okay, don't start kissing my ass. It takes only one hour in Hollywood. What's to explain? Everybody's got a boss."

Now I wanted to recoup and was ashamed it was necessary. "That's what I need, I guess."

"Okay. Okay."

"Did you read the story I sent you?"

"No," said Zernbach. "I don't read scripts until I am told the nut."

"What do I do, then?" I asked, puzzled. "Do I tell the plot?"

"Try this," Zernbach said. "A man walks into an office where three men are talking. What can he say that makes the others immediately suspicious of each other?"

"He says, 'Which one of you wanted a bodyguard?' "

"No good. Old hat. Old Henry."

"Okay," I said. "He walks in and says, without looking straight at anyone, 'I'm sorry. I thought you were alone. I've got the mother outside.' "

"Better."

"Can I come to see you at the studio?"

"Come next week. Where did you send your story?"

"To your office. It wasn't complete, just a teaser."

"Don't knock it," said Zernbach. "Some teasers are better than the picture."

The manuscript I sent to Zernbach he never did read, not even after I started working at RKO, only part time, for one hundred fifty a week. I was told by Formayev, who was nominally my boss at the studio, that movie scripts like mine tend to be derivative. New writers, he said, look for successful precedents—plots or characters or dialog that are reminiscent of hits. That way they hope to win a hearing from producers.

My script began with a private "Op" who sits in a San Francisco hotel bar, his face lighted off and on by the neon words "Hi-Ball." He gets a call to go to an expensive apartment on Polk and finds there a Eurasian-looking woman who sits with her ankles crossed the way short people do. She says a man named Vasili has a certain passport. The Op doesn't ask if it's hers, because why would you want anybody else's passport? To pay for it he's told to pick up a thousand dollars at a bank on Montgomery Street with a certified check, but instead he goes straight to the address, a hotel on Garland Street, where the landlady is wearing a pillowcase as a turban and slops a mop on his shoes and tells him she don't want no trouble and he says, "Then don't let your hair down." He tries the knob and inside finds this guy with a purple throat, garroted, his cheap coat gathered under his shoulders. When the Op snakes a piece of cardboard out of the lining of a suitcase in the closet, it's not the passport but a photograph of his client and the dead guy in earlier days. He leaves by the fire escape. Back in his office he gets a call to meet his client at the Ferry Building, but there he finds a man in an expensive suit who asks him right off why he didn't pick up the thousand. The Op is carrying the *Examiner* with a headline about Vasili ear to ear and says, "Let's stop throwing pennies. You set me up. I don't take money blind. Medicines neither. Vasili was going to kill me or I was supposed to take the rap for his murder." The dresser denies it and says the Op's client wants to see him again. The Op agrees but he first tails the dresser to the Japanese consulate; then he goes back to Polk, where the doorman says nobody like the Eurasian woman ever lived there, and when he heads for the Federal Building he's almost run down by a carefully driven car. He figures now he's a bad insurance risk, so he cashes the check and assumes he'll be followed from the Montgomery Street bank, as he is. He doubles back on the tail, knocks him out, and frisking him finds a Daly City address. In Daly City he meets a girl who takes him for somebody else and he plays along without knowing for sure she's suckering him. Besides, she looks great and is immediately friendly. The girl leads him to a place on Grant in Chinatown, where he's just in time to shoot the dresser and find his client wearing a manicure of bamboo sticks and rigor mortis; in turn, he is shot at by guys in suits and fedoras who are Treasury. The Japs are found with counterfeit plates; they were black-mailing the Eurasian to help them. Vasili was free-lancing both the Op's client and the Japs. The Feds wanted the Op out of their play. The Japs sent the girl to bring the Op in because they figured his client had told him all. And the girl, well, she was a real hard case who set up Vasili, who was her father but she didn't know it, and the Eurasian, who was her mother and she knew it. The Op is not surprised, just confirmed in his usual regret, and walks off with a suit that needs cleaning and pressing, a smoking gun, a thousand bucks, and no thanks.

Nor was Lelia Dawson surprised when I told her, some five weeks after I moved into her employ, that I had found part-time work and extra money at RKO. Of course, she had given me Zernbach's address. I was able to go to the studio about nine and quit at two, in time to meet Arthur when he arrived home in the school's Ford station wagon and stay with him until his bedtime, although I was now less energetic in playing games and inventing personae, but Arthur was unnoticing out of hopefulness. Lelia would sometimes ask about the studio when I sat with her on nights when she was back late from working or partying: it got to be a habit, her ringing me up at the cottage as late as midnight. "Do you want some buttermilk?" She often looked exhausted, her refreshed make-up unable to repair effects of many hours under klieg lights, her elegantly almond-shaped eyes closing deliberately as she made an effort to shake off recollections of a tiring day. By now I recognized that Lelia took the effort to remain constant.

After I made a mess of her first party, she did not comment except to say, "Thank you for defending my house," and immediately she invited me to another party, which included most of the same people except, of course, my goggle-eyed victim and the woman who called me a Nazi.

"You like Formayev?"

"He's bright."

"John, you don't mind my asking: how is it you seem not inclined to regard Hollywood and Los Angeles as unnatural? You do see some of the same things I do, don't you?"

"I don't know many places. But it seems to me that things are critical in themselves. Out here things are clean and new; the buildings are original; nature is original. When Arthur and I go up to Mulholland Drive, I feel like saying, 'Yes, this is the way it's supposed to be.' "

"What is?"

"I don't know: whatever I expect. America."

"And you expected it here?"

"I think I did. There's room out here, as there is where I grew up, but there's also work. With work there's the chance of good and bad things happening, although I don't see too much bad here. People drink too much. They may cheat. They fool around. But it doesn't amount to much. It's not really evil."

"Why not?" Lelia leaned forward, a circlet of hair uncurling over her right eye. She struck me as earnestly beautiful.

"Well, the stakes are low. What's at issue here? Not war and peace."

"The Hollywood illusion is supposed to be dangerous. Life isn't the way it is in the movies."

"I guess not, Lelia. As a matter of fact, life is not the way it is." I paused, embarrassed. "All simple statements about life," I continued, "are not very useful. Whether they're true or false, you can choose."

"I don't want to choose," Lelia said, lowering her head, "not tonight anyway. I don't want to grow old, but I shall. I don't want to imagine what Arthur's life can become, but I will. I don't want you to leave for a while longer, but you may."

"Well, I've succeeded in having no plans. I can make it at the studio with Formayev, I'm pretty sure. I never see Zernbach except for his coming by twice to hit me in the small of the back and say, 'What do you hear from the East?' "

"Is that your telling him that his orders come from New York?"

"Yes. He didn't like it."

"You must learn to hold some things back. Good night, John."

Probably Lelia was right. I do find it difficult to converse under constraint. Only recently have I rid myself of envying those people who seem wise because they are taciturn, when in fact I've discovered that most of them are stolidly uninformed. Fortunately, Formayev talked incessantly and only expected me to be lively in response. The RKO bull pen of junior writers, copywriters, researchers, and translators he ran like a seminar; he could be seen in one cubicle or another cajoling and scolding and finally wearying of his subordinates like a teacher who is suspicious of his ultimate reward.

The RKO studio in Hollywood was cramped, the main offices and sound stages and lots thrown together so that the wardrobe storage, writers' offices, and electrical and

paint shops were found in unplanned, incidental alleyways. On the boulevard the studio looked spacious behind
its white flat front and corner fluting and the double-
stroke letters whose style was popular just a few years ago:

R·K·O RADIO PICTURES.

Every morning I looked up at the studio logo, the ball of
earth surmounted by a radio tower that on all four sides
signals the studio call letters. Formayev said this mark was
fitting because movies are the only imperial enterprise in
the United States, sending films instead of consuls to hea-
then lands. He characterized everybody, running down a
hall or into an office, a small and skinny figure, his vest
open and his shirt glittering with ash from chain smoking,
calling to the "opiate workers of the world."

"You know what the movies do for Americans like you
and me?" Formayev asked me once, typically urging me
out of my desk chair so he could occupy it.

"Wait a minute," I replied before he could continue.
"Just who are you and me this morning?"

"We are the huddled masses, just off the boat at Ellis
Island."

"Okay."

"What movies do is give us a reference. We will always
be able to stay in touch because we saw the same pictures.
We all went with Ronald Colman to a far, far better place;
we all reached for that butterfly with Lew Ayres."

"By the way, Formayev," I said, "I know that you are
spelling that r-e-f-e-r-e-n-t-s because this is a very classy
discourse."

"I was spelling that word classy when you were standing in rice paddies."

"The Good Earth."

"See what I mean?"

What an enormous number of movies have I seen! Like most kids from laboring families, I saw a lot from the time I was seven. Saturdays I would see triple features running from one o'clock to after five-thirty. By the time I was twelve or thirteen I would check the "Ten Best Movies of the Year" list published in the local paper against my attendance. The inventory of remembered movies made it difficult to rewrite scripts I was assigned: the original dialog, and my own rewriting, seemed plagiaristic, or at least reminiscent. I was asked to fix up bits of dialog, though only once asked for story ideas and never assigned to put a novel or play into a screenplay.

About three weeks after I started working I met a woman who fifteen years earlier wrote captions for the silent movies. I told her of my unease over being unoriginal. She said it was cured by telling every story, however simple, as if it were the only one in the world. It was not a bad prescription. I liked her comment that in the silent movies the goal of the writer of dialog was to cause an actor's eyes to widen, narrow, sparkle, lower, grow misty, or go blank. "In fact," she said, "in the silents you soon learned that an audience watches the actor's eyes even when he is being shot or is shooting someone else."

Maybe it confirms Formayev's notion that screenplays are fundamentally different from drama. He and others argued against making dialog "literary," allowing a sentence to grow beyond twelve words and using similes and metaphors, this especially because if style intrudes, it forces the staging of scenes. Despite these injunctions, there were successful novelists and dramatists hired at large salaries to sit in the studio offices. The paradox was resolved, or I thought so when I realized that the name of the game was reconstruction and rewriting. I was not ever in the game, I realize now. Formayev never praised my work. Nor did he ridicule it.

Chapter

15

Sitting around the writers' offices could be engaging, especially when Formayev was in and out, but there were awkward occasions. One of the writers was dependably drunk from eleven o'clock on. He kept going with alternate dollops of gin, which he carelessly secreted in his wastebasket, and a Thermos of coffee filled by one of Formayev's secretaries, whom he called his "batwoman." He named me "Sir John" and reported to strangers that I had won a "technical knockout over a blind midget" in Lelia's house. Some of the writers and researchers were easygoing, but also ambitious to talk familiarly with novelists and dramatists in residence at RKO who were nationally known. I must say that I shared their desire, but the swift-changing traffic through the studio and my own short workday made it improbable that I could get to know published authors very well. I wanted especially to talk with Raymond Chandler, who lived at Pacific Palisades and came to RKO the summer of 1941 to screen his book *Farewell, My Lovely*, which I read the year before when Father Oliver lent it to me. I admired his stories in the *Black Mask* issues I bought assiduously along with

Dime Detective during my college days. My script about the private detective owed a lot—if not the whole—to Chandler and to current detective suspense pictures. *The Maltese Falcon* I saw four times that year. Lelia told me that RKO had bought *Farewell, My Lovely* outright for not much money and was making two pictures out of the same book. By the time I left Hollywood I realized it was so. It may be that Chandler was paid a salary, as are all writers who are under the Writers Guild contracts. It was the same I was given, mine being for six months only. Formayev said that Chandler had finished a new book but otherwise was reticent about him.

Now that I think on it, Formayev did not really talk about people precisely or intimately, whether they were in the studio or outside. He characterized everyone by nicknames or in generic terms roughly pertinent to their movie credits. Mostly he liked to talk about the movies as a kind of manufacture quite apart from its famous people. I think he could not quite accept that motion pictures were sought as creative works. He devised a theory that they began as an extension of retail merchandising, that the nickelodeons were stores where the owner could show and sell "shelf goods." As businesses, movies had not much to do with the legitimate theater. Indeed, Formayev suggested by his remarks, however flippant or serious on the occasion, that movies had only a tangential connection with drama. "The main thing, if you get down to it, is that a movie is put into a can. Sure as hell movies are a kind of machining, and they are sold by studios to theaters the same way auto companies sell to their dealerships." I suppose in large part I was impressed by this theorizing because Formayev spoke of the movies like a phenomenologist. I told him that once. He said, "Don't

182

tell the head office. They'll fire me for practicing medicine."

About this time I noticed articles in serious magazines about movie-making—they were a new criticism—that tried to explain its success apart from accepted notions of entertainment in vaudeville and circuses. Formayev scorned the proposal now familiarly advanced that Americans need celebrities to suffice for the lack of traditional aristocracy. "What did we do in the way of ritual adulation before 1910?" he rejoined. But he did not argue against Hollywood as a place where myths could be made. I told him there were no Icelandic sagas in Ohio. He was intrigued by my saying that it might be possible to find out exactly who invented the American mythical heroes we all were taught in elementary school, John Bunyan and Pecos Pete and a John Henry sort of figure I particularly discounted, a Slavic steelworker who was said to have wrought mighty deeds of strength and daring in the Pittsburgh mills. I told Formayev that one of the few times as a boy that I contradicted a teacher openly was to say that such formulations were plainly suspect. I thought them condescending in the same manner as my being asked time and time again, even as a college freshman, to tell the class how Christmas or Easter was celebrated in Serbia.

On the whole Formayev was not encouraged to believe that the movies in their present form would last the century, ascribing his doubt to various technical possibilities, including the transmission of pictures by electric signals at the New York World's Fair in 1939, and the probable development of a compact, cheap projector for showing movies at home. "But you know, killer, what will finally do in this miserable town is not invention but Murdoch."

183

"Murdoch?"

"Nooky. Every goddamned studio boss and producer and director is screwing secretaries, starlets, strangers—daughters and mothers night and day. They'll kill the business. I'm not talking about the Hays Office and the Legion of Decency. That's crap. The movies survive scandal. That they have in common with art. I'm talking about business. I mean real dime and dollar business. Those guys who ran the nickelodeons were damn good businessmen who counted the take and went home to the Bronx or Union City to their fraus and kinder, but these guys running Hollywood now are going soft from sex."

"Is it true what they say about movie stars, Formayev?" I asked, feeding his gasconade.

"Yeah. And it's true what they say about Chinese pussy. Ask any producer. In Hollywood, Krafft-Ebing is considered sentimental."

"I can't believe that sex can break this whole industry," I said.

"I didn't say it was one thing at a time. Anything can break you out here: the money runs out, somebody dies ahead of schedule, a star takes dope. But the crux is age. It's not just the women stars who get old—this is really profound, isn't it?—it's the directors and producers and studio bosses who are afraid it will all end. That's why they behave like tomcats on a hot wire. Listen," Formayev said, holding a cigaret up as if it were a sparkler, "don't believe any explanation about the future that is mainly political."

No one offered explanations of politics to me, in any event. I met some actors and directors and a few scriptwriters who fled from Munich or Vienna or Warsaw to

Paris and thence to Nice to Lisbon to New York—it was a refugee route well known by then. I knew that Thomas Mann lived in Pacific Palisades, and Bertolt Brecht just a short distance away, north of Wilshire somewhere. Viennese accents (and sometimes, as Lelia said, Budapest accents passing for Viennese) were not new in Hollywood; but the refugee artists and writers probably had more influence intellectually here than in the East, judging from what I heard from writers who came from New York. Formayev showed a scorn for those who talked about art as a form of politics and said of Communists like Brecht that they proceeded on a deliberate misreading of history. Odd, he never considered that we suffer our moral respect for history, which is what I thought when talking with Communists I knew back home during the days of the Spanish war.

It was Winterfield who talked to me about politics without vehemence, probably because he did not accept politicians as authorities on fate. I told Winterfield once that Formayev challenged the usual notion that the West gave elbow room to people to be themselves, rugged conservatives, a doubtfully salutary result in any circumstance. Formayev had told me: "That's crap. Those frontier towns were as tight as a cat's ass. What happens when people live in the middle of nowhere? They get together."

"What was his corollary?" asked Winterfield.

I said, "I guess the place where you can be an individual is New York."

"On the grounds that people living close together protect themselves by making each other strangers?" Winterfield said no more except that the Plains Indians were less complicated sociologically and invented sign language so that they could communicate over great distances.

I met him first at Lelia's one late evening when he came to dinner with two of her English friends. One Sunday not long afterward, Lelia and Arthur and I went to his ranch in the canyon that leads down to the beach at Malibu. He invited us to come afternoons whenever it was convenient and so we did, Arthur riding a pony that Winterfield kept along with two gentle mares in his stable while I sat on the coarse lawn that rolled up to the back of the huge house. I drank lemonade out of a frosted glass and squinted, motes dotting my vision, into the afternoon sun. Behind me under the cover of a fringed umbrella Winterfield sat, looking tall even when seated; his wheat-colored wool sports coat hung from his shoulders without a crease and his hands were laid on the silver knob of a polished bamboo walking cane precisely aligned between his knees. Out of doors Winterfield looked in the distance frequently, but in talking he found your eyes directly except when he mused so that an exhausted topic could creep away under the cover of neglect.

I came to stay with Winterfield three weeks after Arthur and I had visited his house for the last time. It was at a second dinner at Lelia's that he invited me to stay with him, on learning that her husband had demanded that Lelia share Arthur over the Christmas recess. She agreed and took the injudicious step (in my view) of sending him to his father in Chicago two weeks before the close of school on the grounds that he would avoid the holiday traffic and could more readily return the day after Christmas. She would then be free of work for almost a month and planned to go to Washington, D.C. at the turn of the new year.

I saw Arthur off at the new Union Station. As we waited for the Sante Fe to board passengers, Lelia and the chauffeur circled Arthur, picking up his dropped while-away presents—a miniature chess set, a small jigsaw puzzle devilishly displaying unvaried blue skies over the Leaning Tower, a coloring book made of vellum, designed for watercolors rather than crayons. He was more encumbered than usual, for Lelia dressed him in Chicago winter clothes. He became anxious when I took his hand to walk to the track, asking me at once to look after the pony at Winterfield's and to calculate his chances of seeing hobos along the tracks. Lelia delivered affectionately conventional instructions and tried to appear unobtrusive as she talked to the conductor and porter. I was surprised that the conductor took her twenty-dollar tip. Inside the train I took Arthur aside and told him to go to the diner early for each meal so that he could be seated without waiting. I repeated this to the porter and gave him five dollars of my own. Soon Arthur was off, waving from the fixed window bravely, his thick hands brushing the glass as if to erase it.

We stopped at various shops on Wilshire coming back: Lelia was buying presents for Christmas. Back home she told the chauffeur to wait while I got clothes from the house, so that he could take me to Winterfield's. When she saw me emerge with my duffel bag and coat hangers held over my shoulder, she was annoyed, no doubt because she had earlier encouraged and praised my buying a suit and three changes of sports clothes, including the first sports coats I owned, and had assumed I would also buy a suitcase to carry them in. It had not occurred to me. She went inside, and it was not until the car had turned off Sunset into Laurel Canyon and then onto Mulholland Drive that I realized I had not asked if she would be home over Christmas and whether I should return then. I did not ask the chauffeur. He considered it a victory—in a game only he played—when he was asked for information about the household. He took me to the house in Malibu Canyon, below which the Pacific looked still and secret at one o'clock on the thirtieth of November, a Sunday. The next week I commuted to the studio, using the smallest and newest of Winterfield's four cars. The next week there was no question of reporting to work.

In the house were a husband and wife who looked after Winterfield, Hungarians who spoke scant English. The man drove his employer to occasions and used a car to shop for food four miles away, but mainly during the day he was busy downstairs and on the patio with a stiff broom for the carpets and a chamois skin for windows. The Hungarians alternated serving meals, the husband at luncheon alone, and both at dinner because of the several courses. Winterfield took his breakfast in the kitchen at a mission table shiny white from enameled paint. Most of the upstairs bedrooms were closed off, as was part of the main floor, including a music room and his wife's morning room, where she had written letters, just like the people in Edith Wharton's novels. Winterfield told me that he had lived alone since his wife died in 1928; before that, they together had been alone since 1910, the year his son left for Fountain Valley preparatory school in Colorado. His daughter, now forty-five and somewhat older than her brother, had not returned except for rare visits since she left to attend a private secondary school at Dobbs Ferry, New York.

Winterfield was born in California, an inheritor of the gold rush. Some settlers jumped from Independence to Sacramento, he said, "clean over the country like hungry frogs," but his own parents arrived in 1853 by schooner after having crossed the Colombian isthmus. "The real gold," he said, "was on top of the land. My father grasped that right off, and started a business of searching titles and insuring real property. He watched so many land booms and busts that he never bought much property himself: he made his money on the turnover. He gave me fifty-five thousand dollars in 1889, when I was twenty-two, and told me to invest entirely on my own."

"Did you pay him back?"

"No. He was not a true Calvinist, even if he was a Scot and a Presbyterian. He did not believe in debts between fathers and sons. Here we pay the price, after all, of ourselves being free."

"Is it so bad?"

"Yes. Sooner or later every parent feels cheated." Winterfield never mentioned his own children, but spoke frequently and easily of his father. He had died, it startled me to realize, in the nineteenth century. I tried to visualize the rococo days his father spent in his last years, attending ceremonies at which ribbons were cut, picks wielded, trowels laid, and keys presented for the hundreds of opening of streets, railroad spurs, and whole blocks of office buildings. This was the era of Huntington, Crocker, Spreckels, and Matson, but Winterfield said that economics is more surely told not by the huge excursions of money but by thousands of fortunes made quietly in law practices, insurance, retail stores, small city newspapers, jobbing. He told me this as we walked slowly on the path that led to his stables around a rock garden and a fish pond fed by water from his own tower, a quarter mile eastward of the house.

I protested that it must have been, all the same, money at times made unexpectedly and spent without precedent; that for his father it must have been momentous, from the first, coming to California.

"Why do you say so?"

"It is the end, going west. California is the end of the line," I said carefully.

"Then it can be no less than Utopia. One does not dream beyond the limit."

"Madmen must."

"They are here, too. It is the last place. It is also the last time."

On Friday I sat with Winterfield at dinner and smoked and talked while he finished eating and drinking white wine. I was so much at ease with him that I did not pace my eating to his own. Winterfield ate quite slowly without, I think, savoring his food. I told him about the studio and, feeling safe, mentioned making Zernbach defensive by introducing the issue of his superiors in New York.

"Do you want power?"

"I don't want to be humiliated," I replied.

"Then you should recognize what power is. It rests not in titles, not even in spending money. It is, ultimately, the authority to transfer funds. Your friend's New York bosses can reduce or increase budgets; take money from one thing and enlarge another. They are able to restrict people without necessarily defeating them."

"In any event, you still have to have the money."

"Or political office, which gives you the use of other people's money."

"Well, it is never unlimited, is it?" I said. "Money runs out. Politicians get voted out of office."

"Yes, but not surprisingly, usually. Men in power usually presage their own defeats."

On Saturday I drove Winterfield in the big Packard to Beverly Hills to look at some paintings. I had never been in an art gallery: before this, it struck me as impermissible to enter unless you were actually prepared to spend money, as I was when I went into a new-book bookstore the first time at age thirteen. Winterfield knew French Impressionist work expertly, as the paintings and books in his house seemed to indicate, and he had a curious business connection to artists that I discovered that day. He owned a number of movie houses that had earlier been either legitimate or vaudeville theaters. In the 1920s he engaged the Parker Decorating Company to renovate them. Parker artists designed plaster-and-gilt wreaths and egg-and-dart ornament on the prosceniums, on the ceilings Beaux Arts scenes; the next decade they stripped this decoration in favor of straight lines marked in glass and metal, contrasting black and white. On their own, a few of the Parker artists showed Winterfield their seascapes and landscapes. We saw some that day and he bought an oil painting by an artist named Puthuff. It was a view of Monterey Bay: cypresses like curtains against the sky. I admired Winterfield's unhurried manner, his not always commenting when a painting was put on an easel by the gallery manager. We ate luncheon in the Beverly Wilshire Hotel in a garden at the back of the lobby. The street and sidewalk were clean and calm and inside the guests showed a not indiscreet demeanor.

We rode back in the thin blue air of a December afternoon. That night Winterfield went to dinner somewhere in Brentwood. I ate from a hot casserole with the Hungarian couple in the kitchen and afterward read a collection of one-act plays written by Susan Glaspell, Lady Gregory, and others. Winterfield's library was a surprise to me. I could not detect a dominant interest. Out of the convention that old people are especially concerned with how lives are spent, I expected to find more biography. I read far into the morning, untired. It was Winterfield himself who woke me, standing straight in the doorway holding his bamboo stick.

"You will want to know immediately. We are at war. Pearl Harbor was bombed by the Japanese."

"How is that possible? It is four or five thousand miles from Japan!"

"From airplane carriers. Perhaps submarines."

"When did it happen?"

"This morning, just before eight, Hawaii time. There is a great loss of life, and eight or nine capital ships. Planes, too, at Hickam Field."

"What will we do?" I was still sitting in bed.

"No doubt we will declare war this evening or tomorrow."

Try as I did, anxiously, I could not visualize the scene at Pearl Harbor. Was the supply depot next to the ship moorings? In any event, Jean would not be at work so early, not before eight, but for her father it might be different. Winterfield returned downstairs to listen to the radio while I dressed and went into the kitchen for coffee. The Hungarians spoke to me nervously and were more solicitous than they had been all week. The woman's eyes were red. Her husband told me urgently, "It is more than

Japanese. It will be the Germans and Italians."

"I know. The Berlin Pact."

"Will America lose?"

I was so startled by this question, which he put genuinely, that I shouted at him that it was in no way a serious issue, that no country could reach the United States, let alone defeat it. "Begin now," I said accusingly, "to believe that we can win any war." When he thanked me, I felt sorry.

That mood did not persist as I re-entered the living room, for Winterfield was quick to assess my elation.

"You feel relieved, don't you?"

"Is it relief? I feel as if there now were great chances. At least I know what to do. I'll enlist or try for an officer's commission."

"You could be wounded, or die."

"That is not really one of the chances. It appears awful but it isn't," I told Winterfield, not wanting to sound callous about the casualties at Pearl Harbor, although in fact I felt no regret, especially after the radio confirmed there were no houses bombed near the harbor or above Waikiki. I thought about the old man at the hotel whose geopolitical theories were now put to trial. I remembered standing at his French windows after one of our talks, looking out to make sure the world was still there, a big blue balloon tied to the Point Loma lighthouse. The old man kept seeking the crux of the world, like the bar on a teeter-totter. Where was it?

"Well," Winterfield continued, "you are now chosen."

"What? I'm sorry."

"You have a team." And he was right, perhaps knowing that it defined part of the intense competitiveness I had felt since the day I entered kindergarten. I always feared failing, though rarely did I exult in succeeding. The worst thing, I discovered early, is not to be asked for. Even on the sandlot you sense the inexorable horror as opposing hands are lapped on the handle of a bat and the pudgy kid already knows he will be the one left last, and then not chosen but consigned.

"When will you go?"

"I'll quit the studio tomorrow and go home to get my official records."

"So soon?"

"Yes. Thank you for asking me here. I will see you, I hope, when I get back. Is it okay if I stay until Tuesday?"

"Of course. You were to stay longer."

When I returned from the patio for dinner I had already telephoned Formayev at his house to say I was quitting. That night I wrote my father to get my birth certificate from the state capitol and find my college transcript in my cardboard file case. I was tense with energy but did not talk much more with Winterfield except to hear his recounting of the damage at Pearl Harbor. We listened to President Roosevelt together.

"Hitler made a mistake," Winterfield said when he turned the knob on the radio and the green light faded. "He made the mistake of organizing his enemies."

Chapter
16

It was not because of expense I chose the Greyhound bus instead of taking the Sante Fe through to the Union Pacific. I had more than eleven hundred dollars in money orders in my shirt pocket; the difference in fares was less than fifty dollars. Perhaps I anticipated that in wartime I would ride trains frequently: else, through a recondite shifting of tenses, I was in a hurry to leave but not to arrive. The bus followed the main highway eastward from downtown L.A., passing north of Riverside and descending into the desert at Indio, where there was a supper stop. It was invariably hot; the late sun was orange and cast smudged shadows. I walked past the funeral home and summoned how I had regarded Spider's bizarre accident. I was conscious that at the time Nita had doubted the quality of my regret. On the bus as I went to the back window to squint at Indio fading in the west, it struck me that for Nita and me Spider's death was an unimportant confidence.

I rode another day and night before arriving home at the bus station on Third Street. It was bracing to walk the mile to our house on the light snowfall covering the pavement; flakes were already evaporating in the dry air. I turned into the block past the Business College, noticed that the doors of the rectory and the church were closed against the cold, and on crossing the street in front of our house was thrilled to find my father on a workday sitting in a rocker on the porch, his heavy hat low on his head, his arms crossed in a gesture that betrayed his impatience.

"Zdravo, Tata!" I cried to him in the uncultivated style that allows Serbs to hail one another as if we were all Roman senators. He rose, walked to the steps, and inclined his head slightly as I kissed him.

"So you decided to come home. It took a war," he said in Serbian. "Are you broke?"

"I have more than a thousand dollars. I would have had a couple of thousand more, Tata, if I had known not to bet against four of a kind."

"You do it when you have four higher," he said. "Don't worry about the money. Drop your clothes in the house and we'll go to the Dalmatian's for some ham." He wanted to show me off, as he had done since I was a boy of five or six, to those of his countrymen who could be found downtown—the Dalmatian barkeeper, the Bosnian from whose fruit store we bought pomegranates, the Montenegrins who stayed in a boardinghouse on Front and Second Streets when not working the coal fields. Before we left he insisted that I change my shirt and put on a coat, though harrying me not to unpack completely.

The Dalmatian was delighted to see us, at once breaking into affectionate, imaginative cursing. I went round the bar and kissed him, as I do all older Serbs close to my father whom I knew as a child. We sat at the last booth at the back, our backs to the six pool tables that stood in a row under green glass shades. We fixed open sandwiches from a ham platter that also held goat's cheese, rye bread, and peppers. The Dalmatian put down shot glasses and a pitcher of beer. My father always ate hungrily, but he was an indifferent drinker, explaining it as a result of his early addiction to gambling: you cannot drink and gamble both, he would say, for it ruins the drinking.

"Do you know about Vuk?"

"What?"

"He died. Like the others."

"How did it happen?"

"His chest. It is the Montenegrin disease, the lungs and the heart. If they are not killed in battle, they die at home cursing their breath. Poor Vuk. He did not want to be buried with our people, because he is entitled to the soldier's cemetery out at the Veteran Hospital. You remember that he was in the American Army." How could I not know? Vuk had told me about the Expeditionary Army that occupied Vladivostok after the First World War ended officially. It was from his accounts I had inferred Leonid's escape from the Reds by stowing on a troopship to the States. Vuk came to live in our house—my mother kept roomers, and most of the time boarders, too—about 1928 and he stayed until my mother died, ten years later. Then he moved downtown to a hotel where other Montenegrins gathered during the coal-mine layoffs, one or two of them living on meager disability awards from the state just as Vuk lived on his soldier's pension.

Unlike most Montenegrins, who are tall and powerful, he was rather small and soft-spoken, a graceful figure who wore a gray suit with a vest and, when I was very young, I recall, pearl-gray spats to match his fedora. He was so thin that my mother winced whenever he bent over to kiss me, for she feared tuberculosis. Each morning about

197

ten o'clock he walked six blocks to the coffee shop in a great old hotel called the Belmont, there to drink two cups of coffee at the counter while reading the morning paper. As most of the roomers worked, I would see only Vuk when I left for school and on returning at three-thirty, but it was in the evenings on the porch, when the Serbs in the house and a few downtown visitors could gather, that I joined Vuk in reviewing the fates of armies from 1389 at Kosovo forward through the centuries to those remnant expeditions of the World War in Poland, Smyrna, and Vladivostok. It was my father's conceit that every Montenegrin can recite thousands of lines of Alex-andrine verses from their famous epics. Vuk did not deny it, but he told me that Montenegrin epics were like radio serials, given to minute narration of the comings and go-ings of messengers and other travelers and to the re-peated forecasting and recollection of the same events.

My father was telling our Dalmatian friend of Vuk's relatives in Podgorica in Montenegro when I heard him say, "Son, here. I found these in his suitcase." He pulled from his overcoat a large yellow envelope, from which spilled newspaper clippings neatly trimmed. One showed me in corduroys in elementary school, holding a dictio-nary for having survived the competition in a spelling bee; another at the Board of Education building alongside a girl as "the only all-A students in Morris Junior High School"; another announcing I had won the citywide mathematics prize donated by the utility company.

My father insisted that we have our picture taken to-gether as soon as I had acquired a Navy officer's uniform of blue with brass buttons and gold stripes. During the first hour I wore it, I became flustered when, on the way to the photographer's, I was saluted by a middle-aged soldier. It was only mid-January, yet the streets were already sprinkled with men from Army, Navy, and Marine recruiting squads and from an Army Quartermaster Corps company billeted near the airfield. The photograph was Italianate, strongly tinted, making our large heads and high cheekbones still more prominent and the black Sirovich hair unnaturally shiny. My father insisted that in our pose I clasp my hands so that the single stripes on both arms would show.

On the way home, I told him I'd stop in to see Father Oliver, who had been in the hospital when I returned but was just back in the rectory. My father appeared reticent for a moment before he left me, and it was only after I was in the rectory and had spoken to the housekeeper, Mrs. Bradley, and gone to his bedroom, where he lay next to a window overlooking the atrium, that I realized my father already knew that Father Oliver was dying.

"I don't know what to say. I am sorry."

"It is quite enough, John. Do not think of ceremony. It is the only sensible thing to say under the circumstances."

"I am so very sorry, Father Oliver." He looked at me intently, almost staring. I went on, "Will you go back to the hospital? Is there some kind of treatment?"

"Not for cancer. All I can do is to hope to die well."

"What does it mean?"

"In this instance, not killing yourself. Cancer is excruciatingly painful, I am warned."

"But you believe suicide is a sin."

"Yes, it is a theft from God. I'll manage. I simply do not want to embarrass myself over pain."

"Please don't be needlessly brave," I urged him. "Pain does not mean anything. In psychology I was taught that a being cannot remember pain. It may be the only physical quality that is unmemorable."

"I did not know that. It seems odd I should learn it now."

As I sat in his bedroom watching Father Oliver's face in the thin light of the January afternoon, I wondered why it is so often said that someone's death is "pointless" or "senseless" when in truth all deaths are pointless except in Darwinian meaning. Dying of blood poisoning from a sore on the heel incurred while playing tennis—was it Calvin Coolidge's son?—is not any more pointless than being shot in battle or having your heart stop surprisingly. When Father Oliver asked me, I told him something of this.

"You mustn't so easily deny attributes to fate. Perhaps I mean that you should not consent to randomness, John."

"I suppose randomness helps to explain evil."

"No. Nothing explains evil. I must tell you that when I ascend to heaven I do not expect to find answers to the irrational. It will be disappointing if God turns out to be H. G. Wells."

"Is there anything I can do for you, Father Oliver?"

"No, John. Your being here cheers, though I see you yourself are now engaged at risk. You don't mind my asking how you became an officer so quickly?"

"I applied for a commission in intelligence on the grounds that I read two Slavic languages. Suddenly it came through—only I am not in intelligence; I'm a supply officer, in fact, a paymaster."

"Do you know accounting?"

"Not a bit. I'll have to learn how to keep books, not to speak of how to salute. I've orders to go to the Eleventh Naval District in San Diego."

"But you were there just this summer."

200

"Yes. I am making some sort of circle."

When I left Father Oliver, I started back to the house but stopped in the middle of the street and turned toward the church, entering the nave from the inside storm door that every winter is put up on simple framing. I sat in a back pew and tried to be respectful of Father Oliver's dilemma, but I did not dwell upon anything that was not axiomatic. That night as I lay reading, reassured by my father's heavy, steady snoring, the talk with Father Oliver kept intruding. On the road at Pismo Beach I must have fallen asleep on the sidewalk or the sea wall. For now, at home, I remembered a dream. Someone was dying of congestive heart failure, drowning in his own breath as edema rose in the lungs like water in a column. He said hoarsely, "It's no good to worry. Nothingness is possible. It is simply not known." But I was unconsoled and replied without regard, "I do worry. I am without intimacies. What if they call off culture?" The voice, tired, concluded, "It could happen. Culture is no more than a continuation of experience by other means." I began to shout: "No! No! The Church voted out the pagans. Something must be left for me." The dream ended with whispers of submersion.

I had told Father Oliver that I was making a circle as if that itself was remarkable. But the moon makes diadems. Your hair swirls from a fixed point according to hereditary plan. Lost in a wood, you circle left or right. Like an English bowl, once released you show your bent. At Easter my father and I walk round the church three times: the holy numbers are one and three and five and seven and ten and twelve, as Vergil knew leading Dante on planes of ascension. Until it is summed, your number is told in months, solstices, rings of trees. The sun ages you in turns.

I fell asleep dreaming and found myself telling Father Oliver, having crossed the street at the Bible Center and entered the atrium where he stood, that all is harmlessly unknowable, that mysteries are not irregular, just not popular.

"Of course." He laughed. "Purgatory is a parking lot. I'll wait here. You go on, John."

We walked to the Union Pacific station, where I took an afternoon train to Ogden, my father insisting that we walk and he carry the heavier of the pieces of regulation luggage. I could not say good-bye to Father Oliver. When I telephoned Mrs. Bradley at the rectory she told me that he had been returned to the hospital and was "put to sleep for his pain," no doubt given morphine. We walked toward the river viaducts, following my father's choice of a circuitous route. He was immensely proud when in the station I was repeatedly saluted, and smiled familiarly at each encounter. I realized for the first time that he felt redeemed by my being uniformed and reporting to duty. He had not fought formally in a war, and in this was the exception in our family over four generations. It did not count that he had shot at men in America illegally, behind cover. I recognized, too, that we were alike confident and knew tacitly that you may feel lucky in the face of fighting.

Under the four vaults that form the great hall of the station there were signs of adventure: posters warning importantly against loose talk; the hard-heel walk of the MP's and Shore Patrol squads; magazine covers on newsstands showing ships launched and the building of armament; and in small gestures, the proud compliance of a few middle-aged civilian men as they made way for soldiers at the gates.

In San Diego it was still more brisk. Taxis were hard to find, judging from the clutch of people with suitcases on the curb. The old station on Broadway was crowded at midday with sailors and marines waiting for trains that were not yet coupled in the yards. Two new cafés had opened next to the station, and the price of lunch had risen to eighty-five cents. I checked the luggage and walked to the Naval District Headquarters Building at the docks not far away. After three hours of waiting on a succession of yeomen and listening to the loudspeaker's demand, "Now hear this," at least every two minutes, I was given orders to report to Cameron Island to the Supply Officer, United States Naval Air Station, on February 16, 1942. By the time I recovered my bags it was too late to report at Cameron and too late to find an inexpensive hotel, so I settled for paying six-fifty for the night at the El Cortez on the hill. I looked out at the bay: especially because of the blackout, I could see plainly the white furrows of waves on the spit. It startled me that I had not thought of Jean since I returned.

The next morning I was the sole officer waiting on the dock dressed in blues. I felt the warmth and newness of the heavyweight serge cloth. The other officers wore khakis, with shoulder boards on their jackets and insignia on shirt collars. As the whaleboat approached, I stood back in deference to a three-striped commander without noticing that other officers had since boarded. "Well, Pay," he said, "if you don't move your butt, the war will stop. Let me tell you something that will stand you the rest of your life: the senior man is last in and first out." It was the first time I heard the nickname for supply officers, and was somewhat consoled by it. As we approached Cameron, heading into a dock alongside a wooden runway for flying boats, one of the lieutenants said to me, "Just soak your braid in brine. You'll look like a sea dog, just off North Atlantic duty."

Cameron was connected to the island by a causeway but was smaller, most of it landfill used to form slips and drydocks and ground for barracks and supply buildings and two runways, one of which simulated the landing deck of a carrier. About a half mile from the causeway's Marine post was the Bachelor Officers' Quarters, where I stayed the three months before I went to Port Hueneme and for another month on my return. Two strings of rooms faced across a narrow corridor that ran to a wardroom at one end, and, at the other, to a rec room and junior officers' bar. Two officers, in rank from ensign to lieutenant senior grade, were assigned to a room. All my roommates were transients—Navy and Marine fliers who came to Cameron for a final brushup of only two weeks before shipping to Hawaii or Australia.

During the daytime watch and occasionally on night duty I was linked to a long chain of logistics, directing sailors and civilians in an old warehouse where there were rows of wooden propellers and metal struts for planes that would never fly, and in a nearby newer warehouse where cold-weather gear was held, destined for the Aleutians. Within days I was properly addressing seniors and could fill out Supply Corps forms and verify single-entry accounts. The second week I even managed to march a squad of sailors alongside two thousand others in white leggings carrying parade rifles with white straps, past the hawklike presence of Admiral King.

I soon found I had no occasion to return to the island. At the hotel I was told that Harry was already in Pearl Harbor, quickly summoned, no doubt owing to his engineering skills. Nita was in Las Vegas running a liquor store, I was told reliably by one of the old room-service waiters, who was a survivor of the crew that had rapidly dispersed after Christmas. The small woman at the employment office pretended not to know me but responded to my questions about Leonid: he had quit in mid-January and left no forwarding address for mail, of which there was none anyway. I did not go to the Greek's and could not ask of Dolores because no message could go to her uninterpreted by anyone who knew us both. Neither of the older Fanchers was in view, though they worked at the hotel as usual, but George was in the Navy at Bremerton, the waiter told me gratuitously.

I found Harry's house on the island and rang the doorbell. His wife turned on the porch light and talked to me through the screen door. "I'm John Sirovich, Mrs. Gustafson."

"I didn't know you were an officer."

"Neither did I until a month or so ago." But she did not invite me in. "Harry is in Pearl Harbor?"

"Yes. He went two months ago."

"I seem to have missed everyone. Do you know the Fanchers?"

"Yes. No. I mean, I know who they are."

"Do you have any way of knowing where the young Mrs. Fancher is? Her name is Jean."

"Harry told me."

"Told you where she was?"

"That, too. He wrote last week. He saw her in Pearl, working."

I thanked her for Harry's Honolulu address, which I wrote on the back of a laundry slip that I waved, since I had mislaid my pass, at the marine standing at the causeway gate.

I found my roommate lying drunk on his bunk, murmuring to himself. His T-shirt was plastered to his chest despite the agitation of the stale air by a small fan. He seemed not to notice my return. Down the hall I heard the jukebox and I thought about the Mexican girls walking along a Salinas street last June. Across the hall was a voice, a glass sounding. My roommate sat up, rubbing his close-cropped blond head.

"Do you know that a lot of afternoons I been buzzing a house in Dago?"

"No, I didn't."

"That was to remind her I was coming to spend the night."

"Who?"

"The wife of a commander overseas."

"Good."

"No. This is my last night. I'm shipping out."

"That's too bad."

"Too bad is right. You know something? She gets proper when it's good-bye. The commander's wife never sees any of us the last night." He laughed and lay back on the bunk, taking up the fan and facing it as though it were a shaving mirror. "The last night the commander is always number one. That's the funny part. And the rest of us are two, three, four, and keep counting. You see the funny part, don't you?" In the morning he was gone.

Chapter

17

It was early May. The air was light and the traffic was heavy on Cameron Island on fine days when I rose at seven to the sounds of engines to take the eight-to-four watch at the supply office. Routine as was the walk from the BOQ across the runways to the office, I felt inspirited, singled, by shards of light that struck through the morning sky. I remembered that the sisters at the hotel had told me that the first thing they noticed on coming to America, even in New York, was the vastness of the sky. It was to them providential. Cameron was in full swing, sending each week hundreds of pilots to the Pacific, mostly to Australia for staging the recapture of Pacific islands. In the barracks were transient Seabees, naval air engineers, and civilian inspectors who saw to the fitting out of planes and ships that on leaving the bay would move north to the Seabees' headquarters at Port Hueneme and, farther, to Mare Island and Bremerton for final furbishing. Occasionally I went to San Diego to the Consolidated factory near Lindbergh Field, for I had become practiced in collecting gear to supply the Catalina flying boats.

On one trip I saw a former waiter from the hotel, who

was now a riveter. When I asked vaguely if he had heard from anyone, he said Harry Gustafson was home from Pearl Harbor. But I wasn't able to get back to the island to see Harry, for immediately I flew out of Lindbergh on a Catalina, a PBY–5A, up to Port Hueneme, where we landed in a bad chop that scared everybody on board except the pilot. For several weeks I was in PBY's flying out of Hueneme and was soon, like others, calling the plane "Dumbo." Crewmen likened it to a big old family car best suited for a slow drive on Sundays. Its two twelve-hundred-horsepower engines, mounted on the wing above the fuselage, made it ungainly and possibly under-powered even for the slow task of patrolling against sur-face ships and submarines. To land it, a pilot at Bremerton told me, "What you do, see, is to fly it straight into the water at full speed, such as it is." The unvaried if queru-lous affection the PBY was given by pilots must have come from its reputation of never failing.

Coming back from Port Hueneme, I caught a ride on a Navy bus to Los Angeles that went through the cut the coast highway makes in volcanic rock at Point Mugu. I heard the shells exploding on a firing range, but from the sound I couldn't tell whether they were air or surface guns. I do not know guns. During the first days at Cam-eron, I had gone aboard a cargo ship that was being con-verted to an aircraft carrier. The construction was un-believably crude, a forest of steel stanchions rising from the main deck to hold a flight platform off which light planes might rise and, if their pilots were sensible, never return. I stood at the stern staring at a three-inch gun mounted there to sweep against rear attacks, but its range was limited to about twenty degrees either way because two of the new stanchions flanked it closely. "That's a bit strange, isn't it?" I asked a line officer who stood nearby and who was asking me for a supply of kapok preservers, and he replied, "Not if you consider that the gun was in place before the flight deck was put up."

The bus turned onto Santa Monica Boulevard headed downtown, but I got off early and walked in the soft sunlight over to Wilshire, where the RKO studios were. The guard at the gate was somebody new. I had to wait for one of Formayev's secretaries, the one that the drunken writer called his "batwoman," to come down to identify me. "It's you, okay, John," she said wryly, "but there's something different about you." I followed her through the alleyways to the second-floor office, where I passed new secretaries and writers, new to me at least, until I came upon Formayev himself, seated behind someone's desk in a small cubicle, holding in one hand a cigaret, the other twirling his eyeglasses slowly as he looked blankly at the wall of a sound stage opposite.

"What are you dreaming of? Xanadu?" I asked him.

"No. Kansas City. I see that you went in ten easy lessons from gob to admiral."

"I thought I'd come by to explain my sudden departure."

"Well, Pearl Harbor was hardly a secret—except to our own generals and admirals. Anyway, I always cast you for a hero. Where are you now? Or will that betray the Alamo to the Rumanians? We are at war with Rumania, aren't we?"

"The answers in backward sequence are yes, we are fighting against Rumanians wherever they can be found, and I'm stationed in San Diego at the Naval Air Station. Pretty soon I go to Boston for officer's training."

"Are you an impostor, then?"

"No, but I'll go to school to make my stripe legitimate."

"Don't knock it if it's patriotic. Every script going through here now has got a Jewish soldier from Brooklyn, a blond Protestant, and an Irish kid from Chicago who wears a Christopher medal with his ID tag. Once in a while, we slip in a Negro soldier just to stick it to Hitler."

"How is Zernbach?"

"He has four producers working for him. He doesn't ask about you. As a matter of fact, he doesn't ask about me."

"Tell him I'm grateful he gave me the job. I left without talking to him."

"Why don't you just thank Lelia? Leave us out of it."

"What do you mean?" I said, startled.

"Now, don't stiff me. You know you'd never have had the job without her forcing Zernbach. He had no choice. Probably you didn't either."

"You little son of a bitch," I said in a low voice.

Formayey jumped up, trembling. "Listen, Zernbach told me that Lelia's contract was being negotiated. The front office wasn't turning her down." He got behind the chair, cornering himself, for I stood between the desk and the door.

"And what did you make of it?"

"Listen, I figured you for being good in the sack, what else?" He lit another cigaret, peering at me over the match so that he wouldn't lose track of my movements.

"You are expert on sex, Formayev. Or is it just voyeurism? It's a low skill, whatever you're paid for."

"So? So you got paid for nothing!" he said, bolder now that my voice seemed to him at a usual pitch.

"What has money to do with it? I was working because I thought it counted. Whatever you need to do well counts. This war counts."

210

"I don't owe you. Not that goddamn uniform, for sure!"

I went over to the desk, stepped around the chair. Formayev dropped his cigaret and it careened off his vest. Raising his hands protectively, he made a strange bleating sound. He was crying as I left, brushing past his secretary, who had come running in. When I got to the gate, one of the guards stepped out, his hand on his pistol butt. I said to him, "You silly son of a bitch, if you take one step toward me, I'll beat in your head with your own gun. Get out of my way." He moved aside.

I don't remember walking all the way to Sunset and to Lelia's house. I tripped the electric gate latch from memory—Arthur had taught me how to bypass it without a key the first day—and went to the side door where the kitchen opened onto the path. The cook saw me through the door, looked frightened and then puzzled, and only recognized me when I took off my officer's cap. She was effusive and offered me cake and milk while she told me rapidly that Lelia was away on location, not saying where, and that Arthur was still in Chicago because his father had persuaded Lelia to let him finish the year's schooling there. He would be picked up by Lelia at the end of May and they were then to go to Washington, D.C. to stay with his grandmother. It was all settled, she said, as if to ward off the possibility of my effecting a change. I wrote a note to Lelia, another to Arthur, and left them with the cook. I told her, thinking to ensure their delivery, that I would not be in Los Angeles again.

"Dear Gila Junction: I missed you at the hobo jungle on Sunset. The boys tell me you are at the UP yards in Chicago. I sure hope you got through the winter okay. I joined the Navy. It is the biggest hoboing of all. I haven't been to sea yet, but I've flown up and down the coast in a big seaplane. When the war is over, Art, I'll come back to see you. You'll be grown then and maybe we can hit the road together, all the way on the Great Northern to where the Mountain Men still live. I won't tell you to be smart at school. You will be, anyway. Just try to grow up not too fast. Your friend, Carson City, also known as Ensign John Sirovich, United States Naval Reserve."

"Dear Lelia: The first time we met, at the hotel, I almost had to punch an actor-waiter who is now a friend to keep him from impersonating me for the sake of a tip. At my first party in your house I hit Marty; and just today when I stopped by the studio to thank Zernbach I scared poor Formayev. I'm not proud to relate it. He told me you made the studio give me the writing job, and yes, he assumed that intimacies were rendered. I don't think he knew why I scared him—I didn't hit him, nor did I intend to, whatever you may hear. He was cynical about my work and he assumed I was, too. I know my grave fault. I want everything to make a difference in my life. Maybe I don't understand what kind of difference I make in other people's lives. I hope I did right by Arthur.

"I am glad, our being friends. I'm sure you meant to be kind in making the studio give me the job, but it was not right really, because now I'll never probably find out whether I could be good in making movies. I'll soon be leaving San Diego, where I am a naval officer. I joined up in December and left Mr. Winterfield's to go home two days after Pearl Harbor. I think now that I was all along waiting for the war, though I detest suffering in people who can't fight back. I guess I'd like you to think me tolerant even when I am unaware. John."

Back on Cameron I was greeted by another new roommate. For three nights I drew the four-to-four watch, logging the reports of my chiefs, whose crews manned the supply docks and warehouses. On my own hook, I kept open the disbursing office so that men departing early could draw pay and allowances if they returned late from liberty, for right off I had noticed paper work pile up needlessly as current-pay-account balances had to be transferred to Pacific commands. I did not see Harry until the fourth day, when I found him at home after supper on the front-porch swing, drinking coffee from a mug. He looked tanned, thinner, younger. I was surprised to see him in civvies.

"The war agrees with you, Harry. It seems so for everyone except casualties."

"There were a lot at Pearl six months ago. Some will never be reached. I've been cutting away topsides of sunk ships with the Bureau of Docks guys, except those that aren't a hazard like the *Arizona.*"

"Where do you stay?"

"I've come back to move my family to Pearl. I've signed on as a G-14 civilian."

"Jean said nothing would be the same."

"You knew that, too, Big John."

"How is she, Harry? She and her father weren't in the bombing?"

"No. They were okay. She looks fine. She and her dad —he's a warrant officer now—live in a house back from Waikiki. She works at the PX. She gave me a letter." He reached inside his shirt and handed it over. "Listen, John." He leaned forward, stopping the motion of the swing. "That's a nice girl—Jean. She'll make somebody other than George a good wife, but you should think twice whether it's you."

"She doesn't say that, does she?"

"I don't know what she says. But I do know that you want a lot."

"Harry, when are you leaving?" I could think of nothing else to say.

"Tomorrow." He stood up and walked me down to the curb; his wife had been standing at the screen door impatiently. We stopped under the light like strangers sharing a match. "Maybe I'll see you in Pearl if you come through," Harry said, holding the ball of my shoulder in his big hand.

"Or else I'll see you back here after the war."

"I don't think so. You'll be okay, John."

"Thanks. Harry, it seems a million months."

"It was." He turned and I took my time walking back to Cameron, forewarned.

"Dear Johnny: Harry will tell you he's seen me working here at the PX. It seems strange that you are on Cameron not far from the hotel. Remember when the streetcar stopped at the causeway to pick up sailors? I'm really proud that you are an officer. Harry's wife wrote him she saw you. I don't know what to say except I love you, Johnny. I'll always love you, whatever happens. I hope you will remember me young. This letter sounds strange in a way. I don't want it to.

"I am still married to George. I cannot file for a divorce here because I have to go back to the States to do that— the base lawyer told me it. Nita told me that if I go to Nevada, I can stay with her. She is in Las Vegas, maybe you know that. I keep thinking it would be awful if my dad shipped out and I went to the States just as you came through Pearl Harbor! I want you to know that I'm not counting on anything. I guess it isn't going to work out for us. I'm glad you found me when you needed a nice girl so badly. I think I will never feel old or sorry. I'm giving you my address. I want to know if you are safe.

"Remember that day we were in San Diego in the little park? When the sailors were on liberty? You told me that the women stood. They were right. Ever, Jean."

The BOQ was quiet that night. I put the letter down, went up the corridor to the junior officers' bar, sat near two marine fliers who were making those planing motions with flatly joined hands that now are a cliché in movies. I drank two beers. I don't remember what the jukebox played. In the middle of the night I awoke, as if on a signal, to read the letter again, shading the light from my sleeping roommate. I was enduring strong emotion, unable to find its analog. Whom had I told that things that happen to you are like yourself? It was Nita, that night in Indio. Jean's letter was a eulogy to a short unfixed past now wholly hers. By no clever definition could I find my own hand in the motion of her releasing my life and youth while in some certain way constraining her own. I conceived a desire to be free of my persona. In the last wakeful moment I said to myself: You know, don't you, that your present personality is really not much to lose. Death is not important to the future. It is the memory of living lost that exacts. Days and weeks and months you can reckon, not centuries. If pain is not remembered, then you suffer only the unrequited.

Two days later I received orders to leave the naval air station on June fifth, no earlier than 1200 hours, and to report to the Naval Supply School at the Harvard University School of Business in Boston, Massachusetts, no later than June tenth. It gave me no leave time to go home: the best I could manage would be to see my father between trains. I resolved to go up to Los Angeles to gain a few hours, though the route in track miles through Phoenix was shorter. For some reason I decided to pick up my ticket in San Diego, although I could have waited on a yeoman who regularly handled transport. As I emerged from the station and walked south down Broadway I heard my name called in Serbian. "Jovan! Jovan!" Standing in the doorway of a luggage shop, slouched against the back, wearing a cloth cap that looked intentionally too big for him, was Leonid.

"Leonid! Where on earth have you been!" I put my hands on his shoulders and started to draw him into the street, assuming we could proceed to a café or bar, but Leon resisted. "Why are you here?" I continued. "Nobody at the hotel knew where you were. Why did you leave?"

"Johnny, I had to leave. I am alien. I cannot register. I have no papers. I am illegal."

"Well, Leon, let's talk about it. You can't be in danger, I think. They cannot deport you in wartime."

"It's not so easy," Leon said, looking quickly into the street with a constant watchfulness. "They put Japs in camps. Some are citizens."

I persuaded him to walk up to Sixth, where we both knew a Greek who ran a small restaurant. Once eating, Leonid was calmer. He told me he was hurt when I left the hotel without seeing him, but Harry made him accept that I had to go immediately. After Pearl Harbor he found himself anxious over his status but was fearful to consult an attorney, having been told by someone that in America all lawyers are officers of the court. Hearing talk on the radio of alien registration, he took off for Fresno and later Seattle, as if homing toward Alaska as a one-time part of his homeland; and in Seattle he ran into a seaman, a former hotel busboy, who told Leon he'd seen me on Cameron. He returned to San Diego on this information, although I cannot believe he was confident I would be passing by on Broadway one midday. Still, there was something properly Chekhovian in it: times occur.

"Leon, how old are you?"

"Why you ask, Johnny? They put me in jail any age."

"Leonid, how old?"

"I am forty-four."

"You can be thirty-nine. What you've got to do is join the Navy as a cook. Once you've served a hitch, you are automatically a citizen."

"How do I prove I came here?"

"Just say you came through New Orleans, not knowing any English, and don't have papers. You lost them. They won't check, because you'll be enlisting. Real chefs are in great demand in commanding officers' houses on bases."

"What if they don't believe?"

"Give my name. Better still, I'll write Naval Headquarters in Los Angeles this afternoon, vouching for you. An officer I know can make sure it gets to the right person: he's a full Captain in the regular Navy. I'll need your address."

"I've got not much money, Johnny."

"That is the least of your problems." We arranged it right there. I took Leonid to the station, gave him fifty dollars. He gave me the address of a rooming house in East L.A. where I could write him. I was due back at Cameron but stayed with him until he boarded the train coach, carrying his small Gladstone, his pockets bulging with sandwiches, his cap pulled down over his ears. He smiled. You make a secret, you make a friend.

Chapter

18

When it was time, my orders came due, I left the BOQ in a jeep for the short ride to the dock next to the ramp for Catalinas. On the whaleboat ferrying over to San Diego I was the last to board. Within ninety minutes I sat in a train, looking out the dirty coach windows at towns that now seemed too quiet in the midday, as if on a signal deserted of young men. These places looked in some manner different, perhaps less tentative, from the ones last year when I was hitching rides south from San Francisco. Of course, each place was original to me then. On the hillside near Scott Creek I saw firs like umbrellas of mourners descending in the rain, and, farther on, cubes of hay on a distant plateau. I saw artichokes running to the sea where the hills flattened and the shore resigned its oddities. I will not forget those June days coming down into Santa Cruz, where a spidery barn stood weathered away, a web of uneven studs and splintered planks, and into Watsonville, where I felt immediately introduced on seeing buildings named Lettunich and Kalich and Marionvich, several with the year 1911 engraved on stone façades with heavy serifs.

I had spent the night in the Wall Street Inn, A.D. 1911, and out of excitement unspecified I went into the main street before dawn to wait for a ride. It was still dark when a truck picked me up. At a place called Slough I could barely see the boats tied below the coast road across from a stand of elephant palms, but the hills blued and came clear as I was let off at Salinas. I stood on the crumbling gray stones of the highway's edge. Before me lay fields of black loam with low crowns of greenery, rows running together in the distance like railroad tracks and made finite by my perspective. I was breathless for a few seconds. I know now I was holding a vision just then, nothing awesome, not anything more than a scene that was ineluctably mine. Once before it had happened. When I was a boy my mother covered me with a feather quilt and I turned on my side and looked out the window steadily at a Ford car parked in the snow, its wheels scalloped in white, the air darker than the street. Dogmatically I knew it was right; it could not appear any other way.

Coming down the California coast that June I was content that everything was accustomed. On the foot-high sidewalks in Salinas I walked past civic buildings with arches cut through ocher walls, past filling stations that sold local beer inside, little bungalows on the main street and lime-green beauty parlors and Aladdin movie houses. I approved them all. Had all this been set for my benefit just so, a Potemkin village, that I might rejoice in the way people live? I laughed out loud and the Mexican girls in the Saturday-red dresses looked at me.

When the train entered Los Angeles I had four hours to wait before boarding the overnight Pullman on the Sante Fe. After checking my bags, I set out walking, crossing the Los Angeles River, reminded of the many movies I'd seen the past five years that showed its vast concrete sloping sides and narrow bottom. I was looking for Leonid's address in Boyle Heights in the Irish neighborhood, and found the rooming house but not Leonid. The landlady, a short heavy woman of about fifty with a florid complexion, told me in an accent derived from both Russian and Polish that Leonid was downtown taking his physical for enlistment in the Navy.

"Do you tell everyone that?" I asked, astonished by her candor.

"No, just you. Leonid said when a tall officer comes, it is you."

"How did you know I was the right one?"

"He said you walk American but look Slavonian and speak English better than Americans. Also, you are very young, very polite." I thanked her and left a note, written on the back of the empty railroad-ticket envelope, wishing Leonid luck in a war he would finally win.

Retracing my way, I came upon a Chinese cemetery and, nearby, as it was marked on a black sign, THE RUSSIAN CEMETERY. It was no larger than half a city block, surrounded by a wire fence with opposite entrances into a bisecting roadway. Next to it was St. Sava's Serbian Eastern Orthodox Church, which I did not enter but whose properties I could surmise from boyhood memories: the small nave with no pews or benches except those placed against the back wall for communicants who are forgiven for having endured so long; and in front the Byzantine screen pierced by three rounded entrances across which the priest, on duty, moves not in secrecy yet in silence, for nothing new can be said in ritual about the nativity and the crucifixion and resurrection. As I walked in the cemetery, I felt bleak reading headstones that bore the names

Zugich and Knezovich and Dakovich and Popovich and seeing that relatives had sometimes noted their birthplaces (Boka Kotorska, Grahova, Lika). I found myself crying in this place where traffic was scarce and, for me, undestined. Why had these Serbs traveled nine thousand miles to die here?

At a score of funerals I had stood by caskets of men who in life were worked out, spent, or still fierce and sometimes angry or mad, like my godfather, who left me the six-shooter. My mother had kept in her top bureau drawer a pearly gray photograph of twenty or so people standing in the Orthodox church next to an open casket inclined from the back so that the dead man's face showed. I was five, dressed like a Russian infantryman in a coat that fell to my ankles with a belt outside, and I held a wool cap respectfully. Behind me stood my mother in a plain black coat and round hat. How beautiful she was! She was thirty then, with her waist-length golden hair braided and coiled tightly into a crown, pale-blue eyes and firm cheeks, a short strong peasant's body that was incongruously quick. I do not remember her at the gravesides when I was very young, though she must have been present. Always I stood at the foot and waited for my father to say: "It is hard to die in an alien land; we do not remember ourselves." If my father had understood my mother's life, which he could not, he might have concluded that we are made aliens by many means.

I left the cemetery and walked briskly through the downtown business section until I reached the end of Sunset, the other end from the Sunset in Hollywood, and here came upon Aimee Semple McPherson's Angelus Temple, the Church of the Foursquare Gospel. I saw it once with Arthur after we persuaded the Balt chauffeur to drive down Glendale Boulevard so that we could see the big red streetcars disappear into the tunnel that let them emerge downtown. But now I walked slowly twice around the building, which curved at one end toward Echo Lake like a great boomerang. Its façade was Greek Revival with certain Moorish incursions, and at the rear it restated its claim to permanence in a colonnade more or less copied from the Baths of Caracalla. In such a place the imperious, however hopeful, however absurd, can be divined. But you can also trust that nothing popular is banned. It is Four Square, put up in 1923, a decade before the New Deal was declaimed. Americans will accept and can summate anything, I decided as I stood at the back of the temple, so long as they let it run free, for everything ends from its effects. I felt better walking back to the station, a lot better. I boarded the Santa Fe wearing my blues, going east.

My father was waiting on the platform, sweating under his best clothes on a June afternoon, wearing a brushed felt hat and a camel-hair coat that must have been size fifty-two. He stood almost as tall as I but was sixty pounds heavier and greatly stronger. When I was a boy we went each summer to the amusement park to attend the company picnic, the climax of which was a tug of war between the street work gangs of the gas and electric divisions. My father was the anchor man for the gas work gang, and I can see him leaning back, his feet braced against the side of a bunker he'd dug and the hawser tied round his girth, still standing as those in front fell. I would urge him on those occasions to perform a trick no one else we knew could manage, which was to thread a one-inch pipe held in one hand while holding a heavy threader, usually mounted on a steel stanchion, in the other. Now, as the

Pullmans followed the coaches under the glass-and-metal overhang, he waited on the near end of the station platform, strategically but also anxiously placed. His eyes were wet when he turned his head as I kissed him. He picked up my luggage and headed out of the station.

"I have only an hour and a half, Tata."

"I know."

"I'm sorry we haven't time to go home."

"We'll go to the Dalmatian's." And we did. The Dalmatian was not at his bar, but a Serbian who worked for him brought us a platter and shot glasses and beer. Once he asked after my health and destination, he withdrew, and returned but once to refill the glasses. I told my father of visiting the Los Angeles cemetery and of helping Leonid.

"You might have to speak up for me."

"What do you mean?"

"Two FBI men came to see me. They found I take Serbian newspapers."

"Christ! It's not against the Constitution."

"They asked about the Socialist and Communist papers I get from Cleveland and Pittsburgh."

"What did you say?"

"I asked why they weren't interested in the royalist and fascist papers I also take. One tried to make me feel better, I suppose, by saying his father had come from Sweden. I told him, 'I have nothing to say to your father, like I don't to you.'"

"You should have told them you tried to enlist in the Marines."

"The Marines told me I was too old, too heavy. In Serbia it's different; there you fight because you are not in good shape."

"Tata, do you remember Pan Breznewicz?"

"The Polish watchmaker? He used to kiss your mother's hand and say, 'Pana, I regret to tell you that I have been drinking.' She would then lecture him on wasting his life."

"He also would say, 'Pana, I know what my ambitions were. I have forgotten my hopes.' "

"Your mother lectured me all our days. Only I didn't waste my life; rather, hers."

"I cannot argue that," I stated slowly.

"No, you can't. She never understood. I couldn't do better."

"Tata, this is painful. What she didn't do is worse: she didn't approve of your life."

"How does it happen? A man is what you see, not much more."

"She didn't want heroism, Tata. She was the immigrant: she wanted people to learn right, act right, and save. Not like poor Pan Breznewicz, who went to the university in Cracow and in 1910 was sending his friends one-dollar greeting cards with Gibson girls at the opera, and ended up in our town telling his customers to come back next week."

"She would approve of you, John. It is terrible she didn't live to see you like this."

"Well, I'm only an officer. And not forever. Who knows after the war."

"You will stay in the East. There is nothing for you here."

"Maybe it would have been different, Tata, if we had lived in a colony of our people where there are husbands and wives and kids and cars and picnics and lodge meetings and churchgoing and all that, like the Slovaks on the north side or the Poles near the stockyards."

"Maybe. Yes, maybe. We were like an island in this city.

Every house, from Third Street moving away from the river, we were alone, just us and the boarders who moved in and out and the coal miners who came to town."

"Remember when we went to Thermopolis to stay with the Serbian families? You were a character witness at a trial for Slavko."

My father laughed. "Did I do him any good?" In fact he had. Vuk told me our people need folk epics so they'd know how to act extremely. A Montenegrin in one tale pulled a pistol from his sash and put it to the temple of a Moslem; when it misfired the Montenegrin chided the Turk for showing fright, went round a corner to tamp in new powder and wadding, and returned to blow out the Turk's brains. My father's friend Slavko, when his pistol misfired as he aimed at his enemy in a bar, showed no disappointment or anger, went to his rooming house, and returned with another pistol to shoot dead the man, who was incredibly still standing where he'd left him. He was defended by an old lawyer named Walker, who placed a huge hearing-aid box on the table in the courtroom. Whenever he didn't want to hear—like Eugénie Grandet's father in Balzac, he was selectively deaf—he got up and fiddled with the tubes. My father's testimony startled the judge. "You need the law," he said, "but the law is not enough when a man humiliates you, for then you must kill him." When the judge asked my father what he proposed, he was ready: "Judge, put him in jail—it's only fair he go to jail—but not for long because he did no harm to others. The dead man was a bachelor." The judge gave the prisoner ten years. Six years later he showed up at our house looking, as before, distracted and intense. My mother said my father's younger brother looked that way when he put down his gun next to his plate at meals when strangers were present. That was before he sailed from New York with a shipload of Serbian volunteers and was drowned within sight of the Montenegrin shore when an Austrian submarine let loose its torpedo.

"Why are we born volunteers, Tata? Remember I drove Krsto Popich around the coal fields in 1936 when he recruited Serbians and Montenegrins for the Republic in Spain."

"He was a brave man."

"And a Communist."

"He was a Serb."

"Yes. I know he was brave. But it didn't end right. He died in Aragon, an alien land like any other you choose."

"I can't disagree. I don't even understand it. Who do you suppose decides?"

"Your enemies, I think. They choose your battlegrounds. They name your triumphs."

"I think you're right. Hitler will save Stalin, maybe Roosevelt, too, from some failures. He makes everybody look brave, including of course the Germans."

"I cannot tell if I'm brave."

"Take my word, Son. You are. But you will not die in this war, I'm sure."

"I am, too."

"Then, as the Montenegrin poet says, you will have a harder choice, which is how you will die in peace."

"That may depend, I think now, on how I make money."

"It is what your mother would say. All our troubles were over money. She would not understand that money occupies your mind only if you don't have it."

"Sure, Tata, I see that, but I can't say it proves her wrong." She had no use for mixing money with pride, as my father does. He gave unrepayable loans to his people out of her small savings. When I went up to the university it was she who decided, insisted, I would not work a year or two "to help out." She understood the capitalist idea right off, a peasant woman who grasped that money is best saved not against bad luck and then spent in ceremony, but, rather, in favor of good luck, for risk and celerity. She never entered a school door, never held a pen, never was handed a piece of paper by someone who knew she could not read. For all that, it perhaps followed that her faith in learning was firm but rudimentary. She distrusted politics and did not know that intellectuals are excited by power, as scribes have been since they first served pharaohs. How could she know? She was born the subject of Emperor Franz Josef, the youngest of nine children of a mother who died at forty and a father who afterward was drunk in the fields. She emigrated at age thirteen with a tag round her neck naming a mill in Pennsylvania, where she went to operate a loom, then two looms, by running back and forth across an aisle, until she was persuaded to strike by IWW fellow workers and lost her job. She kept boarders in coal camps and later in the city, never ceasing, always respectful of work, only that. She taught me to be not impressed by those whose pride outran their means. She was moralistic: for her nothing was sanctified if not earned.

"Your mother was a good woman," my father said as a matter of fact. I had been staring at the table.

"She came to America too early."

"It is possible. Is it too late for you?"

"No, Tata, I'm in time."

"For what, do you suppose?"

"For whatever I will do. It exists and I will be into it,

probably, before I know exactly."

"Is it that open?"

"I'm sure so. Why else did we come?"

"God knows. Your mother died working hard and not being doctored right. I worked a hundred holes. I spent what little money we had. We were ignorant."

"We were ourselves, Tata. I don't believe in reconstructing fate. And since I left home, since the war started, I don't any more believe in history."

"I killed Mexican scabs during the Ludlow Massacre strike on the hogback west of Walsenburg. I dug and loaded coal in four-foot-high rooms underground near Carbondale and Gebo and Raton. I took orders from Welshmen and others who never heard of Kosovo or Karageorge."

"I know." Then I said, not in defense, "Today in Yugoslavia, had you stayed, you'd be in the mountains dying, maybe for the wrong side, whichever one that is."

"Still, I could choose, couldn't I?"

"Yes."

"You don't have to choose."

"No. I thank you and Mama for that. I have a cause."

"You do," he replied. Then he said, "But you will watch yourself belonging to it."

"The Greek I lost the money to in California said I was a Janissary."

"Thank God not. I hope your children will know you."

And that was the last until we reached the station. I saw him turn away as the train pulled out, his heart heaving. The clean diesel engine made the big turn, climbing out of the river valley after it passed under the viaduct where Nita once stood on a saint's day. I looked at the shallow furrows alongside the tracks in the reduced light and remembered the summer week I drove Miss Carrie Sheldon, my high school history teacher, to visit her brother's family in the old ranch town of Ogallala. She paid me to drive her De Soto and we rode on the glassed concrete highway across gray fields. We reached the town square, fronted by white and Dutch Boy yellow frame houses, just as the lights were coming on and people made ready for supper. I knew those people inside without meeting them. Still, it was not home for me. I was not disquieted, for no place is strange to me in this unsettled nation and none will be finally familiar.

About the Author

William Jovanovich is chairman of Harcourt Brace Jovanovich, Inc. Since he was thirty-four he has managed this publishing (and diversified) company of 7,000 employees (in 1970 the public shareholders introduced his name into the company). He and his wife Martha live in New York's Westchester County and Murray Bay, Quebec. Their elder son is a lawyer in Los Angeles; their younger son is a vice president of the Macmillan Company and their daughter a museum graphics designer, both in New York City. Mr. Jovanovich wrote *Now, Barabbas* (Harper & Row) in 1964 and has since published many essays on education and communication. He was a Regent of the State of New York until 1976, and in 1967 Regent's Professor at Berkeley. As an editor he has worked with Erich Maria Remarque, Hannah Arendt, James Gould Cozzens, Mary McCarthy, Jerzy Kosinski, Diana Trilling, Charles A. Lindbergh, Milovan Djilas, and Leonard Woolf.